His Paradise Wife

TINA MARTIN

As she began closing duties at the shop, Emily made sure her display cases were locked. Then she counted the cash in the register, sealed it in a bank deposit bag and locked the cash drawer. That's when she heard the bell at the door.

"Sorry, we're closed," she said without even looking up to see who'd come in.

"That's too bad. I was looking for another necklace."

Emily looked up and locked eyes with Dante Champion, standing there with his hands in his pockets, looking like he was posing for the cover of GQ Magazine. She remembered his very distinct voice and knew it was him just by the sound of it. By the deep tone and smoothness of it. And did the man really look this good on a daily basis? Every time she laid eyes on him her heart skipped a beat because of his good looks, of course, but mostly because she knew Dante had a thing for her. However, she had nothing for him. So to thwart his would-be purchase, she said, "Well, I already cashed out the register."

His lips curved to form a smile. "Credit it is, then."

HIS PARADISE WIFE

AKNOWLEDGEMENTS

Special thanks to the fans who take the time to read my work. It's truly an honor.

Other books by Tina Martin

Accidental Deception, The Accidental Series, Book 1
Accidental Heartbreak, The Accidental Series, Book 2
Accidental Lovers, The Accidental Series, Book 3
What Donovan Wants, The Accidental Series, Book 4

Dying To Love Her
Dying To Love Her 2
Dying To Love Her 3

The Millionaire's Arranged Marriage (The Alexanders, Book 1)
Watch Me Take Your Girl (The Alexanders, Book 2)
Her Premarital Ex (The Alexanders, Book 3)
The Object of His Obsession (The Alexanders, Book 4)

Secrets On Lake Drive
Can't Just Be His Friend
The Baby Daddy Interviews
Just Like New to the Next Man
Vacation Interrupted
The Crush

For more information about the author and upcoming releases, visit her website at www.tinamartin.net.

HIS PARADISE WIFE

Prologue

Dante Champion sure was fine...

Emily could admit that very easily to herself, but she'd never do such a thing to anyone else, especially not to her best friend, Melanie Summers. When she thought of Dante, the tall, sexy, muscular being that bled testosterone through his pores and wore confidence like his thousand dollar suits, she always remembered this – the last time she saw him. It was a few weeks back, but she could recall the *event* like it had happened yesterday. Dante was just one of those distinguished, rarefied men that a person never forgets. That a woman never forgets.

He'd been walking along the sidewalk by her little boutique on Battery Park Avenue with enough swag to melt ice. It had snowed that week, the last week in April, and the temperature was leveling out at around thirty-five degrees. Emily had been sitting behind the counter on a barstool, sipping on a cup of hot cocoa. Her assistant and friend, Sherita, had stayed home that day since the roads in her neighborhood hadn't been plowed. There was no way she could drive in such treacherous conditions. Therefore, Emily had to perform all the operations of the boutique – including working the register, hanging new items and pricing them. Additionally she had to do closing work that entailed sweeping the floors, wiping down the counter and closing out the cash drawer.

At any rate, Emily couldn't believe it was actually him, Dante Champion, strolling by her store. In the town of Asheville, North Carolina, that simple act was the equivalent to President Obama walking down Pennsylvania Avenue without his security detail. It was just unheard of.

Dante's ten-story office building, the building that he himself owned, was five blocks away. Five cold, teeth-chattering blocks. He couldn't be walking to work could he, when he could've easily summoned a taxi or better yet, called his personal driver to swing by in the limo, black Escalade or the Maserati, and pick him up? *Stranger things have happened*, Emily thought to herself. *Maybe the man just felt like walking.*

Fast forward to six o'clock in the evening...

Emily was bored out of her mind. The store had been slow, so slow that she could count the number of customers she had all day on one hand. She'd yawned and stretched enough times to make the Guinness Book of World Records and she caught herself nodding off several times. Too many times. A person could only nod off so many times before they were completely out, and her bed was calling.

"Ugh...is it time to go home yet," she drawled out. Even though it was her store and she could leave any time she wanted, she always made sure to remain open during the regular operating hours that were posted on the door. It was good business practice, one of the pointers that Melvin had given her. He stressed the importance of consistency to maintain validity as a small business owner. He always used to tell her that small business owners were actually big business owners who

2

were just starting out. She believed that and she believed in him.

She sighed, rubbed her eyes until she heard the small bell ringing at the top of the boutique door entrance, alerting her that she had a customer. With tired eyes, she looked up and there stood one of the most sought after men on the Eastern seaboard – Dante Champion – standing six feet tall, dressed in a black business suit covered by an unbuttoned black peacoat with the collars flipped up, enhancing his broad shoulders while drawing attention to his handsome face. Black, leather gloves covered his manly hands and a skull cap fit perfectly on his head.

Emily instantly felt a nervous twinge run through her like a jolt of uncontrolled electricity, but of course she couldn't let Dante see her sweat. He was probably accustomed to the attention he received from women. She imagined that he would feast off of the way women reacted in his presence – women who would instantly become flushed, nervous and nearly drool at the very sight of him. Women who deemed it an honor just to be in close proximity to him. In the same room as him.

Nope. Not her. No way. There was no way she would get caught up under his spell. So she pretended as if his creamy, Werther's Original caramel candy complexion, the result of his African-American, French and Irish heritages, had no effect on her when the truth of the matter was, her mouth was watering uncontrollably for something sweet this very second. Something like caramel.

She nervously cleared her throat, swallowed hard then took a sip of cocoa to satisfy her craving for sugar. She quickly glanced up at Dante walking closer to the counter where she was sitting, then she looked away. She wanted to look up at him once more since he was walking so slowly. Then again, she didn't want to.

Honestly speaking, he was too beautiful to look at and too beautiful to ignore, sort of like staring directly at the sun. Sure, it was a beautiful creation, but one could cause damage to their sight by just gazing upon it.

Dante knew full well the power he had with his handsome appearance. He and his brothers had inherited a bunch of good genes from their parents. Their good looks and features were unique enough to make people inquire about their heritage and stare longingly into their hazel eyes.

Emily, however, maintained her stance on not getting caught in a trance with him. She was tempted to lose herself in his eyes, boy was she tempted, but she pretended to be otherwise engaged on her laptop instead of being hypnotized by his appeal. Besides, there was no need to entertain the thought of being with a Champion man. They were well-known in Asheville for being notorious womanizers and since they were extremely good-looking, successful and had loads of money, women fell at their feet and into their beds as easily as their millions fell into their bank accounts.

Finally, after reaching the counter, Dante greeted her with a simple hello. She spoke to him as well and afterwards, he boldly asked her out to lunch. Meeting his gaze so he could know she meant what she said, Emily declined with a resolute 'no'. When she did, she could see the smirk on Dante's face. He didn't appear defeated when she turned him down, nor did he seem fazed. His look was one of determination, which was something Emily couldn't understand. Why was he so determined to go on a date with her when he could have any woman he wanted? Then it dawned on her. Maybe he'd already *had* every woman he wanted and she was the next woman on his to-do list. If that's what he was thinking, then he was in for a rude awakening because Emily Mitchell was one item on his list that wouldn't get checked off.

Chapter 1

~ * ~

Emily stood up, walked over to the display window and stared out into the street. It was a quiet, boring Monday, and the sidewalks were desolate on the cold, overcast day. Everything appeared gray and dreary and the lack of sun did nothing to improve her mood. To add to the lackluster workday, it was snowing again.

Emily shook her head. She loved snow, but not late-April snow and as she pondered the thought, she watched a few light flurries fall from the sky, settling softly upon the three inches that fell overnight. The only businesses that had opened on the same strip as her boutique was the coffee shop next door and the Caribbean restaurant on the corner. The other businesses, an antique thrift shop, a book store and pharmacy had remained closed.

Irritated with the sound of her own thoughts, Emily took her cell from the coat pocket of her royal blue blazer and dialed her friend Melanie. Melanie was a manager at one of the hotels downtown. Emily was sure to get some sort of entertainment from her. Melanie, no matter what was going on, always seemed to be in a good disposition. She was one of those girlfriends every woman needed – someone to lighten the mood when things were tense, someone who knew how to party when it was time to let loose and someone who had your back when no one else did.

"Guest services. Melanie speaking. How may I help you?"

"Hey, Mel."

"Ooh, girl...I was just about to call you."

Emily grinned, tapping her French-manicured nails against the glass countertop. "And why were you about to call me?"

"Because your man has been all up and through this hotel today, girl. Let me repeat...all up and through...you hear me?"

"My man?" Emily questioned.

"Yes, girlfriend. Yo' man."

Emily rolled her eyes. "I don't know who you're referring to, but need I remind you that I don't have a man."

Melanie smirked. "Try telling him that."

"Okay. I'll bite. Who are you talking about?"

Melanie held the receiver away from her ear, looked at it like she was confused and asked, "Who am I talking about? Em, don't play with me. You know exactly who I'm talking about."

"No, I do not," she replied, though she had a suspicion that Melanie was referring to Dante. Melanie had been a fan of his, pushing Emily to accept a date with him a couple of times before, talking the guy up like he was the next best thing since the merger of fried chicken and Texas Pete hot sauce.

"I'm talking about Dante Cham-pi-on," she said, breaking his last name down by syllables for emphasis. "Remember him? The man who's been after you like a police K-9 on the scent of an escaped convict?"

Emily grinned. "Sure I remember him, but I'm not interested."

"Em—"

"Not interested, Mel. And why has he been *all up and through there* as you put it? Bringing different women in and out...one after another, I imagine."

"No, not at all. He's attending a small business summit that his company sponsored. He's one of the expert panelists, along with other notable businessmen and women in the area. By the way, have you ever heard him speak in a professional setting?"

"No," Emily said, frustrated, ready to hang up the phone. Suddenly her boredom didn't seem so bad after all, especially after all Melanie wanted to talk about was Dante.

"Girl, he's so intelligent, knowledgeable on his subject matter and eloquent. He can convince anyone of anything and that suit he has on is tailored just right to fit that rock hard body of his. Good lawd that man is fine, girl." She fanned herself with a hotel flier.

"Hmm...here's a thought...if you like him so much, why don't you go out with him?"

"Um, hello! The man can't see another woman because his mesmerizing, hazel eyes are locked in on you, Emily Mitchell. You just refuse to accept that he wants you."

"Oh, and I guess I'm supposed to be flattered that one of the Champion men has the hots for me?"

"Yes!" Melanie proclaimed. "You *are* supposed to be flattered. Do you know how many women are after those guys? And instead of accepting any of the women after him, Dante is chasing you, and I'ma tell you straight up...men like Dante are usually the chasee...not the chaser..."

Emily shook her head again and paced the floor in front of the display windows at her store; her black, six-inch stiletto heels drumming against the old hardwood. The Champion brothers were handsome men, but they weren't the only handsome men in all of Asheville. Since Melvin's death, she'd been approached by several men – good-looking, successful men – but she turned every single one of them down. She had no desire to learn the mannerisms of someone else – their likes and dislikes. She'd spent years finding those things out about Melvin, fully immersing herself in his life by being the ideal wife and now, she was alone and lonely with no desire to start over from scratch. So to ease her loneliness, she'd began talking to Armand, a man she met online.

"Em, you there?"

"Yes, I'm here, and just so you know, once and for all time, I'm not about to be one of Dante's flavors of the week or no one else's for that matter."

"Yeah. You would just rather hide behind a computer and chat with strangers instead of being spontaneous and adventurous. What you need to do is put on some hiking boots and climb Dante's peak."

Emily's mouth fell open. "First of all, I'm not climbing Dante's peak or any other man's...peak. Second, Armand is not a stranger. We've been talking for three months."

Melanie smacked her lips. "I really don't understand how you can dismiss a man like Dante for some online guy."

"Very easily," was Emily's answer.

"Yeah, okay...keep on talking to these guys on the internet and see what happens..."

"It's *one* guy, Mel. One."

"That's all it takes for you to get catfished."

Emily's chuckle echoed off the wall of her store. "What exactly does that even mean?"

"It means this man, Arnold—"

"Armand," Emily corrected.

"Whatever. It means he could be someone with a fake identity online. Like for instance, *he* could be a *she*, an old pervert, or a serial killer. Even worse, he could actually look like a catfish."

"And looking like a catfish is worse than being a serial killer?" Emily said through laughter.

Melanie laughed too.

"Oh, you are too much, Melanie. And since when is my love-life the focus of your life? You're single. Go mingle and leave me alone."

Melanie had been involved with a guy by the name of Scott Porter for four years. Before him, she was being dogged out by pretty much every guy she dated and when Scott came along, she knew he was the man she wanted to spend the rest of her life with. That's why, when she caught him red-handed having dinner with a woman, Cheaters-show-style, it broke her heart. She vowed to never trust another man.

"We're not talking about me. Now, back to the issue at hand...have you at least spoken with this guy on the phone yet?"

"No. He prefers chatting and emailing."

"He prefers?" Melanie asked, suspiciously.

"Melanie, cut me some slack, okay. At least I'm trying. You were the one always on my back, telling me that it's time to start dating again and blah, blah, blah...I finally meet someone and you're still not satisfied."

"It's not that I'm not satisfied. I just don't trust this online dating stuff. Why set up a profile online and put yourself out there to the world when there are men...handsome, scrumptious, bachelors right here in this city looking for wives, one of whom is practically begging you to go out with him?"

"Because I think chatting behind the safety of my computer is best for me right now. Besides, there's nothing for you to worry about. I never told you this, but the dating site I'm on is a website created specifically for people who've lost a marriage mate in death."

"Oh," was all Melanie could say. She liked to laugh and joke around with Emily as they always had done since they met at a customer service job eight years ago, but she wouldn't make light of Emily's feelings surrounding Melvin's death. Although the accident that ended his life happened two years ago, Melanie knew that Emily was still very much a grieving widow.

Never had Melanie seen a couple more in love than Emily and Melvin. As the story goes, they'd met in college when Emily was twenty-three, married at twenty-five, and he passed when she was thirty. Those were the best five years of her life – her marriage – and now, at age thirty-two, she was brave enough to chat with a man online. It was a start, especially after she told any and everyone who would listen that Melvin was her soulmate and there would never be another man who she would give her heart to. Another man who could fill Melvin's shoes. Never.

"What website is this?" Melanie inquired.

"It's called Grieving Hearts Connect. They have hundreds of thousands of members with profiles and—"

"Is it free?"

"No. It costs fifty bucks a month. Why do you ask?"

"Because usually people don't play games when they have to pay for something, so I'm relieved to know that there is a charge for it. Have you seen a picture and the profile for...what's his name again?"

"Armand, and yes, I've seen a picture. He's nice-looking...said his wife died years ago."

"How old is he?"

Emily grinned. "You do realize I told you all of this like two months ago."

"Girl, please. You tell me a lot of things on our girl nights, but that doesn't mean I remember any of it."

"Yeah, especially with all that wine you drink."

"If you had to deal with the guests at this hotel, you'd drink too."

Emily smirked. "You better stop talking like that before your boss hears you."

"Girl, I *am* the boss around this joint."

"If you say so." Emily laughed, then looked up when she heard the bell on her door. Two ladies came in, probably from a nearby office building on their lunch breaks.

"Mel, I got customers...I have to go, but stop by tonight so we can finish this discussion."

"Will do. Talk to you later."

Chapter 2

~ * ~

"So I trust your meeting here has been pleasant, Mr. Champion," Melanie said, putting on her professional hat. Even though she knew Dante in passing, she still wanted to maintain a level of professionalism that a man of his caliber would expect, especially when conducting business. Therefore she didn't use his first name when interacting with him.

"Yes it was. Thank you."

He was looking fine as always, smelling good, clean shaven and had a voice that demanded attention.

Mercy...

Quickly blinking and coming to her senses, she said, "Um, you're welcome."

He smiled briefly.

That small act of him smiling nearly took Melanie's breath away. She thought he'd be on his way by now, but he hadn't moved. He remained standing at the desk as if he needed something else? *Did* he need something else? Had she forgotten to give him something? A receipt perhaps?

Dante recalled the last conference they had here two months ago, he'd caught his brother, Dimitrius, ogling Melanie, staring her up and down but he noticed that Dimitrius hadn't said anything to her. Just from interacting with her on a business level, Dante knew Melanie wasn't one of those easy-to-get women. She didn't seem like the type to let a man use her and toss her aside. She had morals and was looking for something deeper, same as her friend Emily. And Melanie was professional, well-dressed and courteous. He wondered what her career background was. She would be a good fit at his corporation.

"Um..." Melanie swallowed hard. "Is there anything else I can help you with Mr. Champion?"

Dante wanted to ask her about Emily, but resisted the urge. Besides, if his plan worked, he'd have Emily Mitchell in his life soon enough. "No, I'm good. Again, thank you for your assistance. It was greatly appreciated."

"You're welcome."

Gripping the handle of his briefcase, Dante walked away from the desk and out of the gold-trimmed revolving glass doors.

Melanie watched him get into the backseat of a black Escalade and close the door.

Dante was a successful entrepreneur of various internet companies, but his corporation's most profitable venture was, Grieving Hearts Connect, an online community dedicated to helping and supporting men and women who'd lost their marital spouses in death. As a part of it, he formed a five-star, resort on Pleasure Island, North Carolina, where widows and widowers could meet and talk with therapists, deal with their issues by comforting each other and using their time in paradise as a springboard to return to their real lives in their home towns with a new perspective and outlook on life.

He formed the company after relocating to Asheville, North Carolina from San Francisco seven years ago. He made the move the same year his wife had passed, convinced his brothers, Dimitrius and Desmond, to come on board with his idea for starting a group of web companies and now, they're all millionaires.

Helping other people who were suffering helped Dante to deal with the loss of Anita – the only woman who had every physical attribute as well as inner qualities that made him want to settle down. He was twenty-eight when they married, but five years later, Anita passed from breast cancer, a disease that her mother had also died from.

After her death, Dante couldn't bring himself to stay in California because everything there reminded him of her – the landmarks, their friends, their house...everything. So he quit his executive position at a top marketing firm there, sold his home and moved away in search of a new beginning.

Once he was settled in Asheville, he and his brothers were the talk of the town. They basically took over the social scene and partygoers knew that if the Champion men weren't at an event, then it wasn't the place to be.

After that partying phase of his life, which he also understood as being the denial stage that Anita was truly gone, Dante began to clean up his image. He missed what he had with Anita and it wasn't until he got his head back on straight that he knew he desired what he'd lost. Unlike his brothers, he wanted love, marriage, a woman to grow old with. Someone to share his life with. The problem was, after all the women he'd met and casually dated, he hadn't run across a woman who could make him *want* to pursue her – someone who could take his breath away.

Then he saw her, Emily Mitchell, showcasing items from her boutique at a community festival. She was one of the vendors there, laughing it up with a customer when her eyes locked with his as he stood a few feet away, admiring her. He was there alone, checking out all the vendors and their products, but when he saw Emily, he stopped and stared, particularly at her full, red lips as she smiled and interacted with customers.

When he noticed her customers were gone, he stopped by her booth and bought a turquoise stone necklace. He told her it was for his niece but he had no such niece. It was just a ploy by him to get her name and number. She handed him a business card that had the name of her shop, Emily's Boutique, as well as her business number, but he wasn't able to get her personal number. He had also been unsuccessful at getting her to go out with him.

Then something amazing happened, almost as if by divine intervention. His brother Dimitrius, head of the accounts department, informed Dante of a new account that had been set up on Grieving Hearts Connect, a woman by the name of Emily Mitchell.

Right away Dante logged onto the site, looked her up and sure enough, it was the same Emily he'd bought the necklace from, the woman who declined his request for a date. Had he communicated with her online as himself, she probably would not have talked to him, and would've easily dismissed him the same way she did when he asked her out. That's when he decided to take on a new persona, to create a profile under the name 'Armand Hill'. He uploaded a fake profile picture – some man's picture he found off of an image search – created a profile and began chatting with Emily.

Over the course of three months, he'd learned pretty much everything about Emily – things that made him even more enamored by her. But he'd grown tired of late night chats and shorthand typing with her. That had gotten old real quick. He needed to *see* her laughing out loud. He wanted to personally tell her, *goodnight*, seal it with a hug and kiss and not by typing 'XO' and logging out of a chat window. He wanted his tongue buried in her mouth while his arms encircled her body. He needed his lady by his side.

So, using his lethal power of persuasion, he devised a scheme to get a ring on her finger by coming up with a first ever, GHC mass wedding at their resort on Pleasure Island. All along, his plan had been to make her fall in love with his online persona, Armand Hill, and he thought he was doing a pretty good job of doing just that – persuading her that he was the man for her, the one who could heal her broken heart. If she accepted his proposal, she would meet him at Pleasure Island. Then and only then would she learn his true identity – that the man she had fallen in love with had been him instead of Armand. In his mind, she'd forgive him for pretending to be someone else and fall hopelessly in love with him. That's how he hoped it would play out, but now he wasn't so sure.

Chapter 3

~ * ~

"Sherita, you may as well go home. It's pretty slow today."

"You sure? I don't want to leave you here by yourself."

"It's fine, Rita...won't be the first time I've been alone between these four teal walls and I'm sure it won't be the last. I'll survive."

"All right, Emily. Oh, and if the roads ice over tonight, I will be a little late tomorrow."

"That's fine. I'm sure I will be too. This April snow is killing me."

"Girl, you and me both. Anyway, hopefully I'll see you tomorrow."

Once Sherita was down the sidewalk, Emily took her laptop from the glass countertop and walked quickly to her back office. She logged into her Grieving Hearts Connect account and signed into messenger.

Armand was online. Emily saw the bright green dot next to his name. That brought a smile to her face. He told her that he stayed online since he spent every day of his life on a computer, describing himself to her as a serial workaholic. That's something he told her he wanted to change about himself. He wanted to settle down and not work so hard, now that he didn't need to.

The thought of him being online and ready to talk to her instantly gave her a feeling of elation. That was a good sign – to feel a level of excitement and a release of endorphins at the mere notion of talking to a potential boyfriend. But was he her boyfriend? Were they in an exclusive online relationship? Those were questions that had never been asked, although they needed to be answered.

Emily rubbed her eyes and wondered how long it would be before Armand noticed she was online today. She didn't message him first because she didn't want to seem desperate and needy. Besides, workaholics, by definition, usually had work to do. However, she didn't want him to think she wasn't interested and excited to jump at the chance to talk to him.

Hmm...what to do, she pondered, balling a fist and resting her chin against it. Then she saw a message window pop up on the screen.

Armand: Hey, you.

The smile that came to her face made her glow more than the bronzer she applied on top of her foundation this morning. She instantly felt her worries ease away.

Emily: Hi, Armand.

Armand: How are you?

Emily: Okay...at the store, bored. It's been dead in here all day

Armand: Probably due to this crazy weather.

Emily: I think you're right. How are you today?

Armand: I'm well, dear. Thanks for asking.

Emily leaned back in her chair. She knew it was

about time they met face-to-face, talked on the phone or called it quits. She didn't want to admit it at the time, but Melanie was right. There was no sense falling for a computer.

Armand: You are especially quiet today.

Emily: Sorry. Just have a lot of things on my mind.

Armand: Like my proposal?

The proposal! How had she forgotten that? Emily clicked over to her email so she could reread the flier that Armand had sent to her. Grieving Hearts Connect was hosting a mass wedding for online lovers who knew they loved each other and was ready to make a commitment. It was taking place this weekend in Pleasure Island, North Carolina at the GHC resort there. After the ceremonies, the newlyweds were to remain at the resort for two weeks where they would receive free marriage counseling, participate in couples grief counseling and group therapy sessions. They would help each other cope with grief, share their stories and learn from each other. A week ago, Armand had asked Emily to take a leap of faith and attend this event with him, in essence asking her to marry him. Today, he was seeking an answer.

Armand: Emily, are you still there?

Emily: Yes.

Armand: The proposal?

Emily: Yes, about that...don't think it's a good idea...

Emily cringed when she typed those words,

knowing that they would disappoint him. Her heart raced, awaiting his response.

Armand: Why not?

Emily: Because we haven't met face-to-face, nor have we spoken to each other on the phone.

Armand: And that bothers you?

Emily frowned. Was he for real? Of course it bothered her! What woman would just marry a man she hadn't even laid eyes on?

Armand: Emily?

Emily: Yes, it does bother me, actually. You know my story...know I have no intentions on remarrying. You know how much Melvin meant to me. We've talked about those things.

Armand: Yes, we did.

Emily: Yet, you're asking me to marry you in a passive way and I've never met you in person. Before I would even consider marrying you, not that I want to get married, but if I did, I would at least need to meet you in person, talk to you...get to know you, Armand.

A minute passed. Then two. Three.

Emily tapped her nails against the desktop, waiting for Armand to respond. She'd told him what was on her mind and wasn't holding anything back. Maybe he was not the kind of man who could accept the truth so bluntly but she needed to be open and honest about this.

Armand: Considering all we've been through, I think we owe it to ourselves to give this a try. I like you.

A lot.

Emily: I like you too, Armand, but I can't just up and marry you.

Armand: Then you have no faith in us or this process.

Emily: It's not that. It's just the fact that I don't know you.

Armand: You know me very thoroughly, Emily, as I know you. We've spent hours communicating about almost every aspect of our lives. You know things about me that my family doesn't know.

Emily: But it's just not the same as talking and interacting in person.

Armand: So you want to end this?

Emily threw her head back in frustration staring up at the ceiling, feeling a sour feeling at the pit of her stomach. She didn't want to walk away from her computer casanova, but she really didn't know him that well. How well can you know someone you've never met? Never spoken with? And why was he pressuring her to get married, knowing her desire never to do so again?

Emily drew in a deep breath, gathering the courage to do what she knew she needed to do – to type the words she needed to say to him.

Emily: Yes. I think that's best. Goodbye, Armand.

Armand: Emily

<Emily is offline.>

Emily folded her laptop closed and buried her face in her hands. She hoped what she had done was for the best, but why did she feel so bad about it?

Sitting at his desk, in his presidential size office on the eleventh floor of the building, Dante formed a steeple with his hands and rested his chin on them while staring at the computer screen – at the last words Emily had typed: *I think that's best. Goodbye, Armand.* He should've stopped while he was ahead and gave Emily a little more time to warm up to him, to *Armand* rather, but he was rushing things because he knew she was the woman he wanted. The quicker he could convince her of that, the better. His plan, however was falling apart and the woman his heart desired was slipping away.

Chapter 4

~ * ~

As soon as Melanie walked into Emily's living room, Emily immediately handed her the flier that Armand sent to her about the mass wedding. Melanie silently looked it over as she sat on the couch.

"So what do you think?" Emily inquired.

"I think it is the absolute, craziest, most ridiculous thing I've ever heard of. Now, with that being said, it may be just the thing you need."

"What?" Emily couldn't believe what she was hearing. She was sure Melanie would have her back on this, especially since she was against online dating.

"Hear me out, Em. According to this flier, you would get married at this resort with other couples, you spend two weeks there, practically in paradise, and then you go home. So you get a man, a marriage and a honeymoon all rolled up into one neat little package."

"Yeah...but there's a problem. Two actually."

"Those being?"

"I never want to get married again, ever. And I don't know this guy."

"Oh, *now* you don't know him, but you've been defending your relationship with Armand for weeks."

"I have, but when you said what you said the other day about how Armand and I have never spoken on the phone, I got nervous. So I brought it up to him again, just to see what would happen, and he just glossed over it."

"Well, you have been talking to him online for three months. You *know* him. You're just getting cold feet, or shall I say, cold fingers." Melanie grinned.

Emily blew a distressing breath. "Okay, it's like this...I feel like I know him, but I don't really know him. And no one could ever replace Melvin. He's my heart and will always be my heart."

"Yes, sweetie, I know but Melvin has been gone for two years now."

Emily's eyes brimmed with tears. "So I'm just supposed to forget about Melvin? Is that what you're telling me?"

"No." Melanie scooted closer to Emily and rested her hand on her forearm. "You'll never forget Melvin. None of us will. He was a good man, but he's gone, Emily. I know it's been hard on you, but you have to let Melvin go and move on. I'm sure he wanted you to be happy. Do you believe that?"

Emily nodded.

"Then this may be the leap of faith you need to find that happiness."

"But what if I don't like Armand in person as much as I like him online?"

"That's just a risk you have to take."

"A pricey risk...if I'm going to do this, I have to sign a contract before I even meet him."

Melanie snapped her head back. "A contract?"

"Yes. That's supposedly how they make you stick to your commitment. So if I change my mind, get cold feet and decide *not* to marry him, I have to pay thirty-thousand dollars."

"To who?"

"To the Grieving Hearts Connect company, and I don't have that kind of money. I'm just barely able to cover the lease payments on the store and business has slowed down drastically—"

"Emily, stop panicking. All you have to do is *not* back out. Do it."

"Gosh...you're such an enabler."

"I'm serious, though. Do it."

"Why? Why should I do this when everything inside of me is telling me not to."

"Because you need this. You need a man, girl. And, not only will you get your groove back. You'll get your parents off your back in the process."

"Well, that's true," Emily agreed, because, as it stood, she couldn't get on the phone with her mother without hearing about how she wanted grandbabies. Her parents were so insensitive to her feelings for Melvin, so much so that they had been trying to set her up with a guy three months after Melvin passed. Three short months!

"Girl, if I hear one more conversation between you and your mother about some grandkids, I'm going to scream."

"So am I," Emily said. Melanie had given her the boost she needed to go through with this, even though doing something this outrageous was so not her. She felt sick again just contemplating it. At the same time, she felt that this might be what she needed to start living again. Besides, she liked Armand. If they could get along online, then surely they could get along and have pleasant conversation face-to-face. Her only concern now was that Armand was who he said he was and not some psycho, preying on lonely, heartbroken women on Grieving Hearts Connect.

Chapter 5

~ * ~

"What's bothering you, Dante?" Desmond, his youngest brother had asked, staring at his brother as he sat in front of his desk for their weekly meeting.

Desmond headed up the marketing department and was focusing all of his attention on the mass wedding event planned for this Saturday at Pleasure Island. He'd drafted a few press releases to review this morning with Dante and Dimitrius. Only problem was, Dante's mind had been elsewhere.

Dante looked at his brother. Yes, something was bothering him. That didn't mean he wanted to talk about it. And he tried to keep up the no-nonsense, hardcore businessman role to hide the fact that he was upset, but his brothers could read him well. Too well. So well that it aggravated Dante to feel their inquisitive eyes on him. So to quell any further interrogation from Desmond, he said, "Nothing's bothering me. I simply want to ensure that the activities this weekend will go as smoothly as possible. This is the first time the company is embarking on an idea as such, so we need to make sure every single detail is handled accurately and appropriately. If we can pull this off, I'm sure monthly subscriptions to the service will increase dramatically."

Desmond nodded. "I got local media on board. Once the ceremony starts, there will be plenty of interest in Grieving Hearts Connect, long after this is over.

Think about it. What we're doing is unprecedented, and people are responding."

Dante nodded.

"Also, I've done some research online," Desmond added. "Seems bloggers have read the fliers on our social media sites and have blogged about it."

"What kind of feedback are they giving?" Dante inquired.

"Well, from the ones I've read, they pretty much had good things to say about the mass wedding, but then, of course, you have negative feedback. Some people seem to think that meeting people online and getting married in untraditional ways will inevitably end in divorce."

"Then they are not changing with the times," Dante said coolly. "People don't just randomly meet at a bar or the supermarket like they did back in the day," he explained.

"Wait...I have to disagree with you on that, my brother," Desmond said. "I met a fine honey at a bar just last night."

Dimitrius chuckled. "What else is new? You're always meeting women, or shall I say twenty-one-year-old party girls."

"You're one to talk," Desmond shot back. "You have a chick on speed dial for every day of the week."

"And yet again, you speak on what you don't know..."

"Okay, let's get back on track," Dante said, short of tapping a pen on his mahogany desk. He'd always been the mediator between his siblings. "Dimitrius, have you seen a spike in membership due to Saturday's event, or is it too soon to tell?"

"Membership has been up twelve percent since the first press releases went out three weeks ago."

"That's excellent. That was a good strategy to send

out a pre-press release, Des."

"I thought it might make a difference," Desmond responded. Removing some papers from a folder, he said, "Now here are the new press releases I drafted up for the local media at Carolina Beach." Desmond handed Dante and Dimitrius a copy. "As soon as you give me the okay, I'm sending these babies out."

Dante placed the press release on his desk, then got up from his seat and walked over to the windows. The reason he came up with this mass marriage idea in the first place had been a selfish one. He wanted to get Emily. He tried to pretend he wasn't upset by the fact that he hadn't heard from her at all on Tuesday and not so far today. He'd been watching his fake 'Armand Hill' profile all day, waiting to see if she would log in and she hadn't.

"Dante, what gives, man?" Dimitrius asked, watching his brother gaze blankly out of the windows. "Thought you'd be more excited than this."

Dante slid his hands in his pockets and turned around to face his brothers. "Emily broke it off with me Monday night, well with my fake online persona but you get what I mean."

"Why? I thought *Armand* was putting his mack down," Desmond quipped.

Ignoring his youngest brother, Dante said, "I think I pushed her too hard, too fast."

"She hasn't been online at all?" Dimitrius inquired.

"No. Monday, she ended things."

"That's a shame," Desmond said, shaking his head. He would never get caught up with one woman when there were so many to pick and choose from. Still, he could understand why his brother had been so taken by Emily. She was a beautiful woman, and from what he knew of her, she was smart, a hard-working business owner and she had eyes that a man could lose himself in over and over again.

"Since you're both here," Dante said, "I want to let you know that I will not be going to Pleasure Island this weekend."

"What?" Desmond said, frowning. "You *have* to go. The media is all geared up to meet the CEO of Grieving Hearts Connect."

"Des, you and Dimitrius will suffice as representatives in my absence."

Dimitrius shook his head. "Dante, I'm with Des on this one, bro. You said you wanted everything to go smoothly...well what kind of press are we going to get once it's known that you're not there?"

"How can I come there when the woman I want to spend the rest of my life with won't be there to accept my ring?" Dante asked in one long, frustrated breath. "I won't do it."

Desmond rubbed his hand across his head in angst.

Dimitrius sighed because he wasn't sure of what else to say. Once Dante had resolved to do something, it was as good as done. The same was true when he hadn't wanted to do something.

"Why didn't you just talk to her? Over the phone, I mean?" Dimitrius inquired.

"Because she would've picked up on my voice and I couldn't risk her finding out that *Armand* is really me. She doesn't like me, remember?"

"Why do you sound like you've given up?" Desmond asked. "Today is Wednesday. The ceremony is Saturday. If you really want this girl, you got today, tomorrow and Friday to convince her to come to Pleasure Island this weekend."

"And how am I supposed to do that when she won't log onto messenger?"

"I got it," Desmond said. "Send her a private message. She doesn't need to be logged onto messenger to get a private message. Send her your phone number and type the words, 'call me'."

Dante shook his head. "I don't want her to pick up on my voice, Des."

"Well, in order to get something you never had before, you have to do something you've never done before. Right? So, send her your number. Once she talks to you for the first time, that has to be all she needs to convince her to be standing on the beach Saturday, ready to exchange vows with you. Now when she gets there and realize that you tricked her, well, you're on your own then, bro."

"I'll think about it," was Dante's response. "Was there anything else we needed to cover today?"

"I don't think so," Dimitrius said.

Desmond spoke up and said, "Don't forget that we need help in the marketing department. I can wait until after the hoopla has died down around the upcoming GHC events, though. Just a reminder."

"Okay," Dante said. "I'll work on it. For now, this meeting is adjourned. I'm sure you both have plenty of work to do."

Dimitrius smirked. "We're sure you do, too."

Chapter 6

~ * ~

If ending things with Armand seemed like the right thing to do, why did she feel so bad about it? Emily had even logged on to her instant messenger on GHC last night and saw that he was offline.

What had she done?

She missed talking to Armand already. In a way, he'd become a distraction from the grief she struggled with after losing Melvin. Now Armand was gone. Or was he? Maybe if she apologized to him for ending things so abruptly, he would be forgiving and they could pick up right where they left off.

Feeling good that this was the right approach, she logged on to her laptop and signed into her profile, noticing a private message indicator light blinking. Before she could click on it, a customer had walked in.

"Good afternoon," Emily said. "Welcome to Emily's Boutique."

"Hi there," the lady responded.

"Can I help you find something?"

"Um...no. I'm just browsing. I'm getting married this weekend and wanted to find a nice vintage piece for my gown."

"Oh, congratulations! That's exciting."

"Thank you."

"Well, we keep pins in the counter display case. Earrings are hanging on the wall as well as necklaces, and there's a scarf rack near the display window."

"Perfect. Thanks."

"No problem," Emily said excited for this woman whom she hadn't known. She remembered how she felt when she married Melvin. It was *her* day – her time to show off her man to the world. There was the dress, bridesmaids, hair, makeup, nails, the shoes – getting married was an exciting time. But to do it all over again, to repeat those vows to another man gave her an unsettling feeling. She had no desire to marry again. She had, however, missed talking with Armand.

She walked over to her customer while she was looking at earrings and asked, "So when is the big day?"

The lady beamed, holding two pairs of earrings in her hand.

"Saturday."

"Girl, you should have your maid honor running these types of errands for you."

"Well, that's the thing...this is going to be a very non-traditional style wedding, so I won't have a maid of honor or bridesmaids."

"Are you getting married at the court house?" Emily questioned. She realized how intrusive and nosy she sounded. She just didn't care.

"Oh, no. I'm getting married at a mass wedding on Pleasure Island this weekend."

Emily's eyes lit up. "Wait...are you getting married at the Grieving Hearts Connect Resort?"

"Yes! You heard about it?"

"I did, actually. I met someone on the site and he asked me to marry him there, but I refused."

"Why?"

"Because I didn't feel I knew him well enough."

"How long have you two been talking?"

"Three months."

"Wow. I've only been chatting with my guy for two

33

months and we decided to take the leap."

"Have you met him in person or spoken with him on the phone?"

"Haven't met, but we talk on the phone every night. He lives in Atlanta. Where does your guy live?"

"He said he was in Charlotte."

"Charlotte? That's a hop, skip and a jump from Asheville...then you're there...and you haven't met?"

"No. He only wanted to chat online and didn't want to meet or talk on the phone, so I recently broke it off, but now I think I was too harsh with my decision. My friend thinks I should go to Pleasure Island and meet him in person. It's like she has this vision of me being whisked into the arms of a prince and living happily ever after."

The woman chuckled as she took another pair of earrings from the rack.

"I'm Emily by the way."

"I'm Audrey. Nice to officially meet you."

"You as well."

"Hey, which pair of earrings should I get?" Audrey asked. "I can't decide."

Emily looked them over for a moment and said, "They all look nice." She only stocked the best merchandise for her store.

"Yeah. Maybe I'll get all of them."

The women giggled.

"So how long have you been a member of GHC?" Emily inquired.

"Um...'bout a year now. When my husband died eight years ago, I had trouble talking to men. A friend of mine told me about the Grieving Hearts site and I made good use of the online therapists there. But I didn't know that I would meet my new soulmate. He's truly amazing and this journey for me has been wonderful."

Audrey had decided to get three pairs of earrings,

and after Emily swiped her credit card and handed it back to her, she asked Audrey, "Was it difficult for you to make that decision to start over and get married again?"

"It was at first, but I realized something." Audrey slid her credit card back in her purse. "I'm responsible for my own happiness. I could choose to be miserable or I could choose to be happy. I chose happiness."

"I like that," Emily said as she handed Audrey a small, logo-imprinted bag.

"Thank you, Emily."

"You're welcome."

"Hope to see you Saturday," Audrey said.

"Maybe you will."

Chapter 7

~ * ~

You are responsible for your own happiness.

Those words that Audrey said earlier resonated deeply within Emily because they were simply true. Since Melvin passed, Emily found many reasons, excuses and opportunities to be unhappy. For a long time, rain made her feel sadness. Made her think of him. Even sports programs brought tears to her eyes since she used to watch football with Melvin.

The only time she could remember having a little slice of happiness since Melvin was when she chatted online with Armand. After talking with Melanie and now, Audrey, she was sure that breaking things off with Armand had to have been a mistake.

At her computer again, she saw the email indicator alert on her GHC home page. She hadn't thought much of it, because she was always getting emails from GHC marketing about events and seminars. Anyway, she clicked on the inbox to open it saw something she hadn't expected – an email from Armand. Right away, she clicked on it to open it. Then she read:

Call me. 555-3429

Emily's heart pounded against her chest like bucket drums being hand-played on New York City streets. Armand wanted her to call him and she couldn't believe it. He'd been adamant against speaking with her on the phone and now, he was offering up his number like a sacrifice. Maybe he realized he didn't want to lose her.

She took her cell phone from her pocket, dialed the number Armand had emailed to her and paused before pressing send, instantly feeling her nerves get the best of her. What if talking to him on the phone wasn't as easy as talking to him on instant messenger? She hadn't thought of that. And to add to the stress, yesterday was the first time in three months that she hadn't had any communication with Armand.

Emily sighed. Then, drawing in a deep breath, she pressed send and braced herself.

* * *

Dante had been sitting at his desk when a call came through on his cell. He knew it was Emily because only his immediate family had access to this number and their numbers were already programmed into his phone. This number wasn't, so it had to be her.

"Hello," he answered.

"Hi, is this...Armand?" Emily asked with caution, butterflies swirling like a tornado in her stomach.

"Yes it is. Is this my Emily?"

My Emily. A big smile came to Emily's face. "Yes, this is Emily."

"You have a beautiful voice, Emily. Makes me wonder why I've waited so long to give you my number."

Emily smiled because she couldn't find words. Talking to Armand over the phone wasn't going to be as easy as she thought it might be. Behind the computer, words flowed easily. On the phone, it was a different story. It almost felt as if Armand was a stranger and not the man she'd gotten to know for three months.

"You there?" he asked.

"Yes. I'm here."

Dante stood up from his desk and walked over near the windows. He kept in mind that he had to alter his voice so she wouldn't pick up on it. He had to be in full 'Armand' mode. "So I know you were pretty upset with me the last time we chatted."

"It was more like I was having a hard time understanding you."

"What don't you understand?"

"I don't get how you can want to marry me when we haven't met."

"Because we *have* met, albeit by unconventional means, but we've gotten acquainted. I actually think we know each other on a higher level than if we'd met face-to-face. We've invested three months into this and I do not wish to throw that away, Emily."

"So where do we go from here?"

"I'm hoping we go to Pleasure Island this weekend so I can finally make you mine."

Emily felt her stomach flutter. Armand was serious and she needed to make up her mind fast. The decision was simple – be happy and marry Armand or be sad and fall into another deep depression for losing Melvin.

You are responsible for your own happiness...

"Emily?"

"Yes?"

"Why are you so quiet? On messenger, you're more talkative."

"I know. I just don't know what to do."

"What does your heart tell you to do, Emily?"

Emily smiled. "My heart tells me to take a leap of faith."

"If that's the case, then your heart and my heart belong together because they are in perfect harmony."

Emily smiled again. Armand sure had a way with

words. "What I *can* say is I'm glad you gave me your number. It's so good to finally hear your voice. It makes you all the more real to me."

"It's nice to hear you say that. By the way, how's your day?"

"It's okay. No complaints. What about you?"

"Business as usual. I'm actually heading into a meeting right now. Since I have your number, I'll give you a call tonight. Also be on the lookout for the contract. I'll send it to your inbox shortly."

"Okay. I'll watch out for it."

"Perfect. Talk to you soon."

Chapter 8

~ * ~

As she began closing duties at the shop, Emily made sure her display cases were locked. Then she counted the cash in the register, sealed it in a bank deposit bag and locked the cash drawer. That's when she heard the bell at the door.

"Sorry, we're closed," she said without even looking up to see who'd come in.

"That's too bad. I was looking for another necklace."

Emily looked up and locked eyes with Dante Champion, standing there with his hands in his pockets, looking like he was posing for the cover of GQ Magazine. She remembered his very distinct voice and knew it was him just by the sound of it. By the deep tone and smoothness of it. And did the man really look this good on a daily basis? Every time she laid eyes on him her heart skipped a beat because of his good looks, of course, but mostly because she knew Dante had a thing for her. However, she had nothing for him. So to thwart his would-be purchase, she said, "Well, I already cashed out the register."

His lips curved to form a smile. "Credit it is, then."

Emily's pulse quickened as she looked at him. He was downright impeccable. Physically, he was the closest thing to perfection she'd ever seen in a man. His smile was beautiful enough to change her mood from a sour one to a more pleasant one, not that she would. Dante, she knew, wasn't really interested in buying a necklace. He was buying some time to be close to her, even if only for a few minutes.

Why didn't I lock the door, she pondered. If she had, she wouldn't have to deal with him and his intimidating aura as his mesmerizing cologne filled the area where he stood in front of her. When he walked away from her to check out the necklace display on the wall, she blew a sigh of relief.

Emily needed to occupy herself and fast. Dante was enticingly fine and that smile of his coupled with those eyes...lawd have mercy. Emily escaped to the back office, grabbed a broom and began sweeping the floor. But with a man like Dante in your presence, it was hard to focus on anything but him. He was dressed sharp again today, in a smoke gray business suit this time with black, leather shoes.

When Dante noticed that she'd been sweeping, he turned his attention away from the necklaces and looked at her, removing his hands from his pockets. "Would you like me to do that for you?"

Eyebrows raised, Emily asked, "Would I like for you to sweep?"

"Yes," he replied with a smirk on his face because she asked the question like sweeping was something foreign to him. "I know how to sweep."

Sure you do. "No thanks. I would hate for you to ruin your suit with a little dust."

"It wouldn't ruin my suit."

"Well, I appreciate the offer, but it's not necessary. I can't have customers in my store working. That's *my* job." Emily resumed sweeping, feeling the heat of Dante's eyes on her.

Dante had been staring as she moved across the floor with the broom, making sure she got every nook and cranny to ensure that her store was clean. And today, she wore a pair of dark, stonewash jeans that hugged her backside just right. "When do you get your next shipment?" he asked her.

She stopped sweeping and looked at him. Failing to withhold exasperation from her voice, she asked, "Shipment of what?"

"Necklaces."

"Next week," she answered. She was surprised he hadn't found anything his niece might like. She also had a suspicion that this niece of his didn't exist.

"So next week?" he said, stalling, wanting to see her lips move while she talked to him. She wore a darker, burgundy lipstick on them today...reminded him of a juicy, sweet, ripe plum that he would like to sink his teeth into and consume shamelessly with uncontrollable greed.

"Yes. Next week. Is there anything else you wanted?"

A smile came to his lips. He wanted a lot – a lot more than she was willing to give. He wanted to put a ring on her finger. He wanted her on her back, in his bed. He wanted her to be the mother of his children. Those were a lot of wants for a woman who wouldn't give him the time of day.

He remembered back to when he met Anita and how defiant she was against him. She hadn't wanted anything to do with him, but being a man who gets what he wants, Dante kept pursuing her until she finally caved. And he married her, but then she fell ill and he watched her die slowly over the course of two years. Now, seven years later, he was ready to start over again. Emily was his target, and he couldn't wait to hit the bull's-eye with his arrow. So looking at her, he said, "May I ask you a question, Emily?"

Emily glanced at her watch. Her store was supposed

to close at seven. The time was 7:14 p.m. She was exhausted, and Dante Champion had a question...

Short of blowing an agitated breath and rolling her eyes, she said, "Make it quick. I have to go," thinking about the phone call she was due to receive from Armand tonight.

"Why do you dislike me?"

Emily's eyes narrowed. "That's your question?"

"Yes. That's my question."

She propped the broom up against the countertop and walked behind the counter, removing a cylinder of anti-bacterial wipes that she kept on a shelf under the register.

All the while, Dante was staring at her, still standing in front of the necklaces with his eyes fixated on her, waiting for an answer to his question.

"Who said I disliked you?" she finally asked.

"I do. Every time I ask you out, you shoot me down."

"Yeah, that's right," she agreed.

"Why is that?"

"Because I don't date arrogant, self-absorbed men."

His smile, that flawless white smile, confused Emily. She just insulted the man and he was still smug about it.

"If that's what you think of me, you got me all wrong," he told her.

"Do I?" she said, wiping the counter.

"Yes. As a matter of fact, you do."

"Well, at any rate, my store is closed, so unless you're buying something..."

"So if I buy something, I can have more of your time? Is that the way this works?"

She sighed.

"In that case, I'll take all the necklaces on that wall."

Emily's mouth fell open. "You can't be serious."

"Dante took his wallet from his back pocket and placed a black credit card on the counter. "I want them all."

Emily sighed heavily. She wouldn't be going home anytime soon, but at the same time, she couldn't complain too much. She hadn't sold this much merchandise in a very long time. "All right," she said walking to the wall and removing six racks of necklaces. After she laid them on the counter, she took a calculator from a drawer and began adding up his purchases.

Dante admired her as she worked. The light pink, long-sleeved blouse she wore went perfectly with her toffee, silky-soft skin tone. He marveled at how her brown, curly hair fell around her shoulders. He wanted to reach out and touch it. Instead, he figured he'd ask her another question, one that was sure to irritate her. Get a rise out of her. "Why won't you go out with me?"

"I answered that question already," she said, angrily punching numbers in the calculator. "Besides, I'm seeing someone."

"I've never seen you with anyone."

"Why would you, unless you've been stalking me?"

"Just an observation," he responded. He certainly wouldn't tell that he had been watching her for quite some time, even learning her daily routine. He knew that she stopped by the coffee shop next to her store every morning for coffee or hot cocoa. He also knew that she closed her store on time every day because she was usually home at her apartment by eight. He knew who her girlfriends were – Sherita and Melanie, and he'd known that Sherita worked at the boutique some days when Emily was otherwise engaged. And since he had been talking to her online under a false persona, he knew other things about her – detailed things that a person would only share with someone they were close to.

Emily added the price of the last necklace and after hitting the equal sign so hard that she could break a nail, she said, "Okay, your total is $684.34."

Dante pushed the card towards her with the tip of his index finger.

"You're really going to buy all of these necklaces?" she asked him again, just to be sure he wanted them.

"Yes."

She picked up his card, swiped it, then ripped off the receipt from the credit card machine, placing it in front of him. She also handed him a pen and when she did, their hands touched. She looked up at him. He was already beaming back at her with his hazel eyes. Just the sensation of his touch made her temperature rise. Made her stomach flutter.

Holding the pen, Dante asked, "So this guy...is it serious?"

"Yes, it is."

"Committed relationship serious, or on the verge of marriage serious?"

"How's that any of your business?"

"Just think a woman like you deserves nothing but the best."

Emily laughed. He had to be kidding, right? The man who'd made his way around women's beds like it was a sport was implying that *he* was the best for *her*. When Emily finally stopped laughing, she asked, "And that's you, I suppose?"

Dante held up both hands in the air. "Guilty as charged."

"Well, I'm not sure what kind of women you've been picking up with this weak game, but it takes more than good looks and money to capture my interest, Mr. Champion. A lot more."

He looked upon her as one would look upon another person in admiration.

Emily frowned again. "Um, can you please sign the receipt. I really have somewhere to be."

"Sure," he said after coming out of a trance. He scribbled his name in an illegible cursive, then handed the receipt to her.

In return, Emily handed him two medium-sized bags. "Here you are. Enjoy your *women's* necklaces," she said, failing to withhold sarcasm from her voice.

"Thank you very much, Emily." He took the bags by the handles and said, "See you soon."

"Excuse me?"

"I said, see you soon."

Don't think so, she thought, watching him saunter away in that sexy stroll that went well with his overall good looks and arrogant persona. As soon as he was on the other side of the door, she locked it and wiped sweat from her forehead. Then she went to the back office, took her keys and purse from the desk before shutting off the lights. Standing at the door, she set the alarm then locked the doors before walking across the parking lot to her car.

Little did she know, Dante had been sitting in his Maserati watching her. Once she made it safely to her car and drove off, he returned back to his office. He had a very important phone call to make.

Chapter 9

~ * ~

"He did what?" Melanie said, her bottom lip nearly scraping the floor.

Emily chuckled. "The man came in my store, after closing mind you, and purchased every single necklace I had in stock." She laughed harder. After pulling herself together, she said, "And he had the nerve to ask me why I didn't like him."

"Oh my gosh...what did you say?"

"I was honest...told him I didn't go for arrogant, self-absorbed men."

Melanie gasped. "You did not say that to him."

"Oh yes I did. And to get him off of my back, I told him I was seeing someone."

Melanie laughed. "Girl, you know you wrong."

"What? I *am* seeing someone. Armand, remember?"

Melanie smacked her lips. "Last I heard, you broke up with your computer love?" Then she started singing the song, *Computer Love*.

"I did, but imagine my surprise when I log onto my GHC account this morning and see an email from Armand, with his phone number, asking me to call him."

"What!"

"Yes, girl."

"Did you call?"

"I did indeed. We talked for ten minutes or so, then he said he had a meeting or something. He's supposed to be calling me tonight."

"And what did you decide about the whole marriage thing?"

"I think I'm going to do it."

Melanie screamed. "Yay! I'm so excited for you."

"I can tell. You almost blew my eardrum out." Emily laughed. Then she heard the call waiting beep, looked at her phone and saw Armand's number. "Mel, it's Armand calling. Gotta go. I'll talk to you later."

"Okay, and you better call me."

"I will."

"I want details, Em. Juicy, delicious details."

"Bye, Mel," Emily said smiling, then clicked over to the other line. "Hello."

"Hi, Emily," Dante said, putting on his 'Armand' persona.

His smooth, manly voice echoed in her mind making a warm feeling come over her body. "Hi, Armand."

"How are you, dear?"

"I'm okay. Just a little tired."

"Long day?" he asked, as if he hadn't known she had closed her store late.

"Yeah. I ended up closing late due to a last minute customer."

"Oh, yeah?"

"Yeah. This guy came in and purchased a bunch of necklaces. How'd your meeting go?"

"It went well," he said, and then, getting down to business, he asked, "Have you had a chance to review our contract?"

"No, I haven't."

"Okay. I was just checking. I know this sounds like a business transaction but I don't want you to feel like what we're about to do is a business deal. I really like you."

"I know. I'm just—"

"Not sure about us?" he finished saying for her.

Emily sighed. "I don't know. I'm so confused about a lot of things and—"

"I have your ring," he said, interrupting her. "I'm holding it in my hand as I sit at my desk, staring at your beautiful profile picture on my computer screen."

"You have a ring?"

"Yes...bought it two weeks after we met."

"Two weeks?"

"Yes, sweetheart. Two weeks. I'm not, nor have I ever been an indecisive man, Emily. I'm a man who knows what he wants and, I...want...you."

Emily closed her eyes and thought about this. She wasn't ready for marriage again, especially not like this, but at the same time, she needed to be responsible enough to avoid playing with someone else's feelings. Armand was putting himself out there and now it was her turn to make a move. "It's almost ten o'clock. What are you still doing at the office?" she decided to ask, to buy her a few more minutes to make up her mind.

"Like I told you a while ago, when my wife died, I immersed myself in my work. I still do. But what I would like to be doing is spending time with someone I care about...someone I can spend my life with. I'm hoping that someone is you, Emily."

A smile came to her already glowing face. "I really like you, too, so I'm willing to give it a shot, Armand."

"Then you'll be there on Saturday?"

"Yes. I will be in Pleasure Island on Saturday."

"You don't know how good it makes me feel to hear you say that."

Emily smiled. "I can hear it in your voice."

"This is wonderful. I can't wait to see you."

"Likewise. Oh, and I'll sign the contracts and send them back to you tonight."

"Excellent. I'm so excited that we're doing this. I hope you are too."

"To be honest with you, I'm scared out of my mind. I feel lightheaded all of a sudden. Are you not the least bit frightened by all of this?"

"No. Not at all. I told you. I know what I want."

Emily blushed.

"And what if it doesn't work out between us?"

After a few moments of silence, he said, "You're counting us out already?"

"No. I'm just being realistic."

"Well, I'm not worried. It'll work out."

Emily sighed. "Okay. I just need to say this. I appreciate your optimism but you should know that I meant what I told you about Melvin. I still love him. I'll always love him. Nothing will ever change that."

"I understand."

"You do?"

"Of course. I still love Anita. I think it's best to keep our deceased spouses safely in our hearts. We will never forget them, sweetie, but we also have to move on with our lives."

"Yeah. You're right."

"So have you picked out a gown yet?"

A gown? A gown! Emily hadn't purchased a gown and with only two days left she had to find one fast.

"Emily?"

"Ah...no, I don't have a gown yet, but I'll get one tomorrow."

"And how are you getting to the coast?"

"I'm driving, I guess."

"Alone?"

"Yes."

"That's a long drive to be going alone."

"It is, but I'm sure I can manage."

"And what if you get tired?"

"I'll take a few breaks...sip on some coffee...it'll be fine."

Emily stood up from her bed, walked to the kitchen, took a glass and filled it with tap water, taking a sip. Armand had been quiet for a few moments. "Hello? Are you there?" she asked.

"Yes, dear. I'm here."

"What are you thinking about?" she asked. "I feel like I can sense your brain churning."

He grinned. "I was thinking that, if you would allow me, I would like to send a limo for you."

"A limo?"

"Yes. I can have one of my drivers pick you up, drive you to the resort and you can rest in the backseat, sip champagne, watch TV or do whatever you want."

"Wow. You have drivers?"

"Yes, I do."

"Business must be good."

"It's okay," he responded, being modest.

"That does sound nice, though. I would love to ride in a limo."

"Perfect. I'll make the arrangements, and so that you're aware, I've already booked our room at the resort. We have the penthouse suite."

"The penthouse suite? You're going all-out for this, huh?"

"Yes, of course. Nothing but the best for my lady."
Emily smiled.

"It's getting late. I should let you go to bed."
"Okay."

"I'll speak with you soon. Goodnight, sweetheart."
"Goodnight, Armand."

Dante poured a little Bourbon in a glass, swished it around and turned it up to his mouth, feeling the heat of the alcohol in his throat. It was only a shot's worth but it helped to settle him as he focused on what he was about to do this weekend. He was going to blindside the woman he wanted, Emily Mitchell, with his presence. How would she react when she found out that the man she'd been interacting with for the last three months online was really him instead?

Chapter 10

~ * ~

Saturday morning – wedding day.

Emily looked around in awe of her surroundings. There were news vans everywhere as well as a crowd of bystanders, likely nearby vacationers from other resorts, taking pictures. The smell of food, the sound of music and sight of beautiful wedding decor put everyone in a celebratory frame of mind.

The temperature today on the beach was a cozy seventy-eight degrees. Unlike Asheville, bright sunny skies were overhead instead of dark, gray ones. A light, warm wind lingered, igniting the feeling of love in the air.

Emily had arrived to the resort last night, so she was fully aware of how magnificent this place was – the place she would be calling home for the next couple of weeks. She hadn't known much about coastal cities, but from what she understood, Pleasure Island was made up of three beaches – Carolina Beach, Kure Beach and Wilmington Beach. She'd had the opportunity to walk the Grieving Hearts Connect resort located on Carolina Beach, and what she discovered was truly amazing: two outdoor pools, one indoor pool, a restaurant and coffee bar, a separate fitness center and whirlpools. The penthouse suite boasted a sixty-inch flat screen TV, an open concept living and dining room, two bathrooms, a private balcony that faced the ocean, his and hers baths, a wet bar with refrigerator, robes, slippers, and a Jacuzzi. On the bed, there was an itinerary for the wedding and activities for the entire two-week journey which included couples counseling every day from 1:00 p.m. to 3:00 p.m., fishing trips, hiking at Carolina Beach State park, paddle boarding lessons and much more.

Now, was the moment that everyone had been waiting for – the marriage ceremony. Emily stood in line, side-by-side with many other brides, waiting for their husbands-to-be to join them out on the beach. With the ocean as their backdrop, the picture of beautiful women in white gowns lined at the shore was a truly breathtaking sight, and with all the media attention surrounding the event, the women felt like royalty. What woman wouldn't want to feel like royalty on her wedding day?

Once pictures were taken of the women, the men appeared, all wearing black tuxedos walking towards their brides and taking them by the hand.

Emily studied the crowd of men, rubbing her sweaty palms together while looking for Armand. She'd only seen his picture online and now she wondered if it was perhaps an old, outdated photo of him since she hadn't seen any man who resembled Armand in this sea of men.

She took a deep breath. Now she was getting nervous. Maybe this wasn't a good idea after all. She'd spoken with a few of the brides last night who had actually met their men in person before coming here. Now she wished she had done the same thing.

Again, she peered at the men, looking for Armand and still, she hadn't seen him. She did, however, recognize one man – Dante Champion – and for some reason, he was walking directly towards her with a smile on his face. What was he doing here?

Emily cringed, broke her trance with him and kept looking for Armand, avoiding Dante at all costs. Still, she could feel him getting closer and closer, the heat of his eyes stalking her.

Dante walked up to her, touched her hand and with a smile on his face, he asked, "Are you ready to do this, dear?"

Chapter 11

~ * ~

The disturbance in Emily's forehead was dominant and defined. She was convinced that Dante had a problem, a serious one. Did he really follow her here? "What do you mean, am I ready?" she asked, snatching her hand away from his grasp.

"To become my wife," he responded.

"Are you delusional? I'm not marrying you. What are you doing here, Dante?"

"I'm Armand, Emily."

"No you're not."

"Yes I am. I'm the man you've been instant messaging online for the last three months and I can prove it." Dante took a picture from his pocket, a picture of some man's face he'd found online to use as his profile picture. He showed it to her.

"That's Armand," Emily said, pointing to the picture.

"No. That's the picture I used on my profile. I found it of the internet. I knew if I used my real picture, you wouldn't have given me the time of day."

Emily's frown deepened. She felt anger build up inside of her. "You're right about that, and I'm not giving you the time of day now." She attempted to take a step away from him, but he grabbed her arm discreetly and gently before she could make a run for it.

With his large hand still holding her hostage, he

said, "Need I remind you that you signed a contract. If you back out now, you owe thirty grand. Do you have that kind of money, Emily?"

Her lips quivered in anger.

"Didn't think so," he said in a cocky, supercilious tone. Then he took charge. "Now here's how this is going to play out. We're *going* to get married. Right here. Right now. We'll spend two weeks on this island and after those two weeks, if you still hate me, as you obviously do now, I'll have my attorney draw up annulment papers. Understood?"

Emily was speechless. All she wanted to do was pack her bags and get as far away from this place as she could.

When she didn't respond, Dante said, "Good."

* * *

The minister welcomed the sea of couples to Pleasure Island, then, after giving a small speech about love and marriage, he instructed the women to face their men and repeat vows. Some women were crying tears of joy. Others had the giggles. Emily wasn't laughing, and if she did begin to cry, they certainly would not be tears of happiness. She was highly upset, so much so that her entire face was a flushed, reddish color and did her brown eyes darken in fury?

Dante reached for her hands and she snatched them away. The mere thought of his hands on her made her skin crawl.

"Are you going to do this or not?" he asked with a smile, finding her defiance comical because he knew he had her right where he wanted her. Once she was settled, he slid a ring on her finger.

Emily felt thoroughly deceived by Dante, but given the present set of circumstances, she wasn't sure how she could back out now. She certainly didn't have thirty-thousand dollars and, with the low sales from her boutique and less than two-thousand dollars in savings, she was already on a path towards becoming heavily in debt.

She looked at Dante and with derision in her voice, she repeated the vows from the minister out of mere rote.

When it was his turn, Dante did the same but not in a rancorous way as she had. He stared happily at her, feeling his heart rate increase since he was finally getting what he wanted. It would've been better had she been happy about this, but he had two full weeks to convince her that he was the man for her. He loved the idea of that challenge with Emily and it certainly would be a challenge, but he would handle her as easily as he did his businesses. If he played his cards right, he was sure to get a huge return on his investment.

Chapter 12

~ * ~

After the ceremony, the couples took group pictures, then private ones before going to a grand reception with open bars, music, dancing and an open mic for brides and grooms to publicly declare their everlasting love for each other.

Dante shared a stiff, first-dance with Emily before taking the mic.

"I just want to say that this ceremony is truly special to me. I never thought I'd be able to find another woman that I wanted to share my life with...a woman that means so much to me. And to my sweet Emily, I want you to know that I will always be there for you and I look forward to spending the rest of our lives together."

Emily couldn't hide the confused look that washed over her face if someone paid her to do so. Was he for real?

As the crowd cheered and clapped after his speech, Dante walked over to Emily, took her right hand and brought it up to his mouth, kissing the smooth skin on the backside of it. Emily flashed a fake smile and when the spotlight was finally off of them, she made a quick run for the nearest bathroom. She slumped over the sink, feeling dizzy for a moment, trying to wrap her head around all of this. Rewinding the events in her head, she tried to come to grips with the fact that Armand wasn't really Armand. There was no Armand. Armand was

Dante Champion. How could she have fallen for this?

Instead of going back to the reception, she headed for the suite. She needed to call Melanie as soon as possible to get some advice and to help her clear her head.

When she stepped in the suite, she noticed Dante's luggage by the door. The room smelled like his cologne.

Ugh...

She continued on to the closest bathroom, peeled the tight, uncomfortable wedding gown off of her body, then took a pair of shorts and a tank top from her suitcase. She sat down on the bed humiliated. Then she dialed Melanie's number.

"Hey, girl," Melanie answered excited. "You already know I have a million questions."

"I know you do..." was Emily's unenthusiastic reply.

"So are you married?"

"Yep...I'm married..."

"I can't believe you went through with it."

"Neither can I."

"So tell me all about Mr. Armand. Is he as dreamy as you thought he'd be?"

"He's definitely a looker. He's so far from what I expected."

Melanie screamed and cheered. "Wait...why am I the one cheering? You don't sound excited at all. Something's wrong? What is it, Emily?"

Emily sighed. "You remember our conversation a few days ago about being catfished?"

"Yeah...don't tell me Armand is an old, toothless man."

"No, it's worse."

"He looks like a catfish?"

"Even worse. Armand is really Dante Champion."

"What!"

Melanie screamed so loud, she left ringing in Emily's ear.

"Yeah...apparently he found some guy's picture online, used it for his profile picture then created an account on Grieving Hearts Connect so he could talk to me."

"Hold up...stop the presses. Are you telling me that the entire three months, you thought you were talking to Armand, it was really Dante Champion the entire time?

"Yep. That's what I'm telling you."

"So you're married to Dante Champion?"

"Dreadfully so."

"Okay...wait," Melanie said, beside herself with excitement. "Tell me exactly how this played out."

Emily took a breath. "All the brides were standing on the beach, then the grooms came walking towards the women, taking their brides by the hand. I was getting worried when I didn't see anyone who resembled Armand and while I'm scanning through the men, desperately looking for *my* man, I see Dante. He was staring at me like I was a T-bone steak, so I quickly looked away. But he walked right up to me, took my hand and, at this point, I'm looking at him like he'd lost his mind. Anyway, he pulls out the profile picture he used online, told me he was the 'Armand' that I had been talking to."

"Oh, that's dirty."

"Tell me about it."

"You could've walked away though. Why'd you still marry him?"

"Because I signed a contract. If I breach the contract, I have to pay thirty-thousand dollars, remember."

"So what are you going to do?"

"I'm going to fulfill the contract terms...stay here with this man for two weeks and when I get back home, this marriage will be immediately annulled."

"Goodness. I knew the man liked you and all, but I didn't think he would do something so sinister and underhanded."

"Yeah, well he did."

"It's almost flattering."

With raised eyebrows, Emily asked, "Flattering how?"

"You know...he likes you so much that he was willing to create a fake profile, talk to you for three months without blowing his cover and convince you to marry him. If you ask me, the man has skills, and for you, my dear, he has a plan."

"Well, I don't see anything about a liar flattering. It's disgusting. I mean, who does he think he is?"

"Guess you'll find out who he *really* is within the next two weeks."

Emily sighed. "You're not helping, Mel."

"Girl, I'm sorry, but given the circumstances, I just think you should make the most out of a bad situation. Have fun, live it up, then come back home and resume your life as normal."

"It's difficult to have fun with a lying stranger."

"Well, technically, he's not a stranger. You've had several conversations with him before. And what has Dante done to you to make you not like him? Well, other than this incident?"

"He's an arrogant womanizer, Mel. You heard the rumors about him and his brothers."

"Yeah, and you're the first to tell me not to believe everything I hear. I think it's time you took your own advice."

Emily shook her head. She could recall overhearing some women in her store talking about one of the Champion brothers – how he'd wined and dined her, slept with her and she never heard from him again. She heard a similar story at the coffee shop next door to her store.

"Well, I'm going to go and figure out where I'll be sleeping tonight," Emily said. "I'll call you later."

"Okay. Later."

Chapter 13

~ * ~

"You're done celebrating?" Dante asked Emily after stepping into the suite. He noticed she had changed out of her gown and into some casual wear as she rested comfortably, her buttery-brown legs stretched out on the expanse of the couch.

"I wasn't celebrating to begin with," she said, snippily.

Dante loosened his bow tie, unbuttoned his crisp, white shirt a couple of buttons down as he walked to the couch where she was resting. He sat on the edge of it near her feet, studying her French-pedicured toenails while his eyes roamed up her legs, to her thighs, her middle, flat stomach, breasts and finally her face.

"Listen, Emily. I know this is a little uncomfortable for you."

"A little?" she said, the heat of her eyes beaming towards him.

"Yes. It's not ideal. I'm aware of your frustration."

"Oh, you have no idea," she hissed, watching him remove silver cuff links and place them on the table. For some reason she was drawn to his hand as he did so, watching how large they were again. Even his knuckles were well-formed and sculpted to perfection. If he wanted, he could punch a hole through a brick wall with those healthy hands.

"Well," he said with a smug look on his face. "Let's make the most of it."

"I'm not making the most of anything."

"Then what are you going to do, Emily? Pout and whine about it?" he asked, mildly amused.

"Excuse me?"

"You heard me. Now while I love to see you pout, because I think it's the cutest thing in the world, I do want you to enjoy this journey with me. So, first things first, we need to figure out where we'll be sleeping."

I'm definitely not sleeping with you if that's what you're thinking, Emily thought to herself.

"I'm sure you've seen the bedroom," Dante said. "I figure you can take the bed and I'll take the couch. For now."

For now?

"Perfect," she said, standing and walking to the bedroom. She shut the door behind her, locked it and sat on the bed, holding her head. Just the thought of being stuck here with Dante made her sick. How was she going to get through two weeks with a man she despised? Then it dawned on her – she'd stay nestled comfortably in this bedroom and would only come out for food. Dante would not have the upper hand in this situation.

Chapter 14

~ * ~

For three days, Emily stayed in the bedroom. As planned, she only came out for food. Dante had tried to talk her into coming to a group therapy session yesterday afternoon, but she refused. She also hadn't attended the new couple meet-and-greet nor had she been in attendance at the first couples bonding activity – tango lessons.

This morning, Emily opened her eyes to find Dante lying next to her with a smile on his face.

She frowned and pulled up the covers over her body. How did he get in her bedroom? She was certain that she had locked the door.

"Good morning, Emily."

"What are you doing in here?" she asked angrily.

"I think it's time we talked."

"No! You need to leave. Get out."

"Emily—"

"Get out!"

"Not until we talk. Now calm down. I just want to talk to you," he said, calmly.

"I don't want to hear anything you have to say." Emily turned around so her back was towards him.

"May I ask why?"

"Because you're a liar. A bold...faced...liar. Every time you open your mouth, you spew out lies."

"That's not true."

"It *is* true! How dare you invade my private life, pretending to be someone else, making up stories about your dead wife. Must've been real entertaining to read the things I wrote about Melvin, huh?"

"Nothing about someone dying is comical."

"You're missing the point! I told you personal things about my life, but you don't care about me or anything I had to endure. All you wanted was to go out with me...the same way you came into my boutique to buy necklaces only so you could get a date with me."

Ignoring her, he said, "Listen...the group will be having breakfast in an hour, then we're all going boating. Why don't you try to make it? You just may have a good time if you get that chip off of your shoulder."

"I doubt that very seriously."

Dante sighed. Had he ever had to deal with a more stubborn woman than Emily? Still, he couldn't deny the feelings he had for her. The first time he laid eyes on her, he'd wanted her and nothing had changed. Even after her resistance, he still wanted her, and when he wanted something, he got it. Point. Blank. Period.

Chapter 15

~ * ~

"Today is the perfect day for this," Dante said, sitting comfortably in the rowboat.

Emily was sitting across from him, facing him, just the way he wanted, only she couldn't stand being this close to the man who had deceived her. She held the oar in her hand and didn't even consider stroking the water with it.

The other couples who'd wanted to rowboat today, about fifteen of them, were already further along than Dante and Emily.

Dante used his oar, sweeping it along the surface of the water, helping the boat to move along with his strength alone. He watched Emily sit there and pout, her arms crossed over her chest now. He laughed internally, then said, "Emily, this is supposed to be a couples building activity."

The sound of his voice irritated her. "Well, we're not a couple, so I don't know why I need to participate."

"Why are you so uptight?"

"I'm not."

"You are, and I think you will feel a lot better if you at least give it a shot. Look around," he said gesturing with his palms up. "Look at this beautiful water on this beautiful day. I'm usually stuck in an office all day and you're busy working in your store. How often do you get a chance to sit in a boat and listen to trickles of water?

Relax, take in the fresh air and enjoy this. Come on. Draw in a deep breath and release it slowly."

He demonstrated his breathing technique while Emily felt her body become tense, increasing her anger.

"How can you do this?" she finally snapped. "How can you be so calm about all of this after you basically tricked me into doing this mess?"

"That's partially your fault."

"My fault?"

"Yes. I would not have *tricked* you into doing anything if you would've just went out on a date with me. I asked you out several times, and you shot me down."

"So you create a fake profile and stalk me?"

His chuckled echoed off the water. "I didn't stalk you. I only created the profile so I could get to know you."

"And you're still lying..."

"I'm being honest, Emily. I wanted to get to know you and, unfortunately, that was the only avenue I had to do that."

"Okay, then answer this...how did you even know I had a profile on Grieving Hearts Connect?"

"Easy. It's my company."

Emily felt faint for a moment. "Grieving Hearts Connect is *your* company?"

"Yes. I own GHC along with several other internet companies. Oh, and for the record, Armand is my middle name." He smiled then winked at her.

Emily took a breath. Dante had been planning this all along. But if he thought she was flattered, he had another thought coming. "Well I had my reasons for not going out with you," she said, "So why not just move on? That's what most men do when they ask a woman out and she declines. Move on. Find another woman to ask out on a date. From what I hear, that's what you do...date around, and I'm not about to be another notch on your bedpost."

Dante erupted in laughter.

Emily rolled her eyes, looked around to see if there was any way possible she could escape being on this boat with him. Heck, she would jump off and swim back to shore if she knew how.

"So that's why you turned me down?" he asked. "You think I'm a womanizer?"

"It's not what I think...it's what everyone says about you."

Dante smirked. "You must have me confused with my brothers, especially Desmond. He's the ladies man."

"Whatever the case, I'm sure a man of your caliber can find another woman to go out with. That's my point."

"Of course I can," he said with confidence.

"Then why don't you?"

"Simple. I don't want to."

"Why not?"

"Because I want you, Emily," he said, giving her a penetrating look.

Emily crossed her arms. "Well, we can't always have everything we want, now can we?"

"I can. I'm a Champion, baby. I always get what I want."

Emily rolled her eyes. "Gosh I hate arrogant men," she mumbled.

"What was that?"

"Nothing," she responded, thinking about Melvin. He was a modest man with not one haughty bone in his body, something she adored about him. Dante, on the other hand, was arrogant and seemed to enjoy getting under her skin.

Looking amused, he asked, "So are you going to

help me row, row, row this boat down the stream or what?"

She looked at him, noticing the sarcastic smirk on his face. "You look like you're doing a good job of it all by yourself."

"Okay, fine. You want to do this the hard way? Let's."

Dante took his hand from the oar and with an intense glare, he looked at her and asked, "What kind of man do you think I am?"

"The kind I don't want."

"Meaning?"

"You're deceitful, a liar, you play on people's weaknesses to get what you want, and while that my work in business, it doesn't work in the real world."

"How did I play on your weakness?"

"You used my tragedy to your advantage. You knew I was having a hard time coping with Melvin's death, but instead of being real with me, you create this fake person and made me believe that I could love again, but it was all lies."

"It wasn't."

"It was!" she yelled, fighting back tears. "Because you don't know anything about what I have to go through. You don't know how it feels to lose someone, a spouse, someone you promised to love for the rest of your life. Yet, you listened to me talk about Melvin and offered me advice like you were genuinely interested in helping me when all you really wanted was a date. So if you don't mind, I want to go back to shore and get off this boat."

After thinking about all she had said, Dante chose not to address her now. She was too upset. "Okay," he responded, and began rowing back to shore, using both oars. He hadn't tried to reason with her because she was too upset to think rationally. But it was time that she stopped being standoffish and short with him and started being open and talking in a more respectful manner. Being on this journey with her for nearly a week hadn't yielded any real results and was basically turning out to be a waste of time and energy. That was about to change.

Chapter 16

~ * ~

In the morning, Emily opened her eyes and laid still on the bed, thinking about how pleasant this trip would be if Melvin was still alive and was lying next to her. She regretted a lot of things when it came to their relationship. They both wanted children, but let their careers get in the way of starting a family. She still liked the idea of having a child, but since she never had a desire to fall in love again, a child was out of the question. She certainly didn't want to raise a child alone.

A knock at the door interrupted her thoughts. She wondered why Dante chose to knock this morning and not just barge in as he'd done the morning prior.

"What is it?" she drawled out.

With the door still closed, he said, "We're having breakfast in ten minutes, followed by a two-hour marriage workshop. I would really like for you to join me." Dante waited for a response, but when she hadn't said anything, he continued, "I'm going to head down there now. Please join me, Emily."

Emily rolled over to look at the clock on the nightstand. The time was 7:50 a.m. Breakfast was at eight and then a marriage workshop was immediately following. She had no interest in neither of them. She rarely ate breakfast and why would she go to a marriage workshop for a marriage she didn't even recognize as being legit or, at the very least, something she'd wanted.

As far as she was concerned, she was still single, this trip was a waste of time and Dante was a pain in her rear end.

Her sight caught the ring that Dante had given her. She left it on the nightstand and hadn't worn it since he slid it on her finger at the ceremony on Saturday. The ring was a glamorous, platinum three-stone, five and a half carat, princess cut diamond, that was as flashy as he was, part of the reason why she refused to wear it. Everything about Dante was ostentatious – from his expensive suits to his arrogant demeanor. Why would she want to be around a man like him? And there was no way she could endure a repeat of the boat incident yesterday, so she decided to spare herself the drama and not join him.

Instead, she got dressed and called Sherita to see how everything was going at the boutique.

"Hey Emily," Sherita answered.

"Hey Sherita. I would've called sooner, but I've been going through a crisis here."

"A crisis?"

"Yes, girl. I'll tell you about it when I get back. How have things been going at the store?"

"Um...it's okay. The shipment of necklaces finally came in and I got them all hung up. Oh, by the way, you sold out of scarves."

"Okay. I'll put in another order now."

"Okay."

"Thank you so much for opening and running the boutique in my absence. I owe you big time."

"You're welcome, girl."

"Okay. I have to go, but I will call you later."

Emily stood up from bed, walked out into the living room where Dante's scent lingered. She stepped out onto the balcony to take in her surroundings, along with a breath of fresh air. This place was beautiful and she couldn't believe Dante owned it.

After calling her supplier for the scarves, she decided to spend the day alone. She headed down to the beach enjoying the warmth of the bright sun as the sparkling sand warmed the bottom of her feet and nestled between her toes. She walked towards the shoreline where the white foam had crested ashore. Seagulls squawked and circled in the air above the water, hunting small fish and seaweed. The sky above was a perfect light blue, decorated with thin, white clouds.

In the distance, a tour boat breezed by and she wondered how she could get on one of those. That would be the perfect thing to do to keep her busy and away from Dante.

After finding out where to sign up from one of the lifeguards on duty, she headed down to the dock where the next tour was due to take off in thirty minutes. She sat, waited and checked her watch. It was a little after eleven. By now, Dante must've realized she wasn't going to be joining him. Maybe he'd finally gotten the hint. He wasn't going to get everything he wanted after all.

Chapter 17

~ * ~

Dante sat alone at the resort restaurant, eating lunch. After Emily hadn't shown up for breakfast or the marriage workshop, he ran back to the room to make sure she was okay, only to find that she wasn't there. He tried to call her phone a few times, but hadn't received an answer.

"What's up, bro?" His brother Desmond asked. He'd seen Dante sitting alone and decided to join him.

"What's up, Des...thought you'd be back in Asheville by now."

"Well, you know, I met a spicy young thang out here and I decided to stick around for a few days."

Dante grinned and shook his head. "What about Dimitrius?"

"He left yesterday."

"Oh. Okay."

"What about you? You good?" Desmond inquired.

"Yeah. I'm cool."

"So what's up with the long face? You've been married for less than a week and you already look miserable. See, that's why y'all crazy folk can have the marriage thing. It ain't for everybody and it definitely ain't for me."

Dante grinned. His brother was a notorious player, but he was sure that there would be some woman to come along and make him change his opinion on marriage.

"Where is wifey anyway?" Desmond inquired.

"I'm not sure at the moment," Dante said, truthfully.

"I saw her heading for the docks earlier."

"Heading for the docks?"

"Yeah. So I would be correct to assume that there's literally trouble in paradise."

Dante wiped his mouth with a napkin. "Emily thinks I'm a liar. She can't seem to get over the fact that I created a profile just to have the ability to interact with her. And you know what...now that I think about it, she's right. I should not have done that."

"I don't know why you did it either. You act like since you're old, you don't have any game."

Dante grinned. "Forty is not old. I'm distinguished, and I can get any woman I want. I tried a different method with Emily because...well, she's...different."

"Different...hmm...that's the same thing you told me about Anita."

Dante nodded.

"Honestly, bro, I thought you said you would never get remarried after Anita died."

"I didn't want to but when I laid eyes on Emily, I knew she had a story and I was right. She doesn't know it yet, but she needs me, just like I need her. I'm not like you...I can't just pick up some chick at a club and bring her back to my crib. Trust me, I've done it before and that doesn't do it for me. I need something stable with a woman I can grow with and spend the rest of my life with. I want children, a family. I want that stability."

"I want those things, too, just not right now."

"That's where we differ. I want that now."

"Well, you got a lot of work to do."

Dante nodded. "When are you heading back?"

"Late this afternoon. I need to get my bag and I'm off to the airport right after." Desmond peeped at his watch. "As a matter of fact, I need to get going." He stood up and pat his brother on the shoulder. "Good luck. See when you get back."

"All right, Des. Take it easy."

* * *

After lunch, Dante stood at the receptionist desk to get an overall feel from his employees on how they thought the event had turned out and if they had received any complaints. There were none.

Afterwards, he returned to the suite, checking to see if Emily was back. She wasn't. He walked in the bedroom, looking around, his eyes instantly fixed on the wedding ring he'd given her. He had the ring designed specifically for her hand. It was special to him. Now it was lying abandoned on the nightstand. Emily wasn't taking him seriously and it irked him to no end.

After taking a short nap on the couch, he woke up to find that she still wasn't there. Or what if she came by while he was resting, then quickly left again? He stood up, stepped out onto the balcony, pacing the space, trying to determine where she might be so he could go looking for her now. That's when he heard the door to the suite close.

He walked back in the living room and saw her making a beeline straight for the bedroom, but she wouldn't escape so easily this time. He'd had enough of being ignored. The woman he fell in love with on the computer was here and he would make her his before this trip was over, starting now.

"Excuse me, Emily," he said, stepping in front of her and blocking her path to the bedroom.

"What?" she asked, feeling a frown form in her forehead, the norm whenever she was face-to-face with him.

"Where were you today? I was waiting for you at breakfast and to participate in the marriage workshops but you never showed."

Emily boldly looked up at the built, broad-shouldered man towering in front of her and said, "I'm not interested in that."

"Well, you need to be. Emily, this is part of the process, okay?"

"What process?" she asked, exasperated.

"What this resort is all about. I formed this place for people who lost spouses in death. The therapists here, as well as all the staff, are well-trained individuals to help people like us to deal with loss."

"People like us..." she hissed. He hadn't lost anyone unless he was starting to believe his own lies. "I don't have time for this. Excuse me."

When he hadn't bothered to move out of her path, Emily looked into his eyes, watching them darken. "Gosh, I really don't have time for this, Dante. Will you please move out of my way?"

"Why do you insist on being angry? I'm trying to work with you and you—"

"You're trying to *work* with me?" she asked, cutting him off. "Newsflash...I didn't ask for, nor do I need your help or anything else from you for that matter."

"Stop!" he yelled, grabbing her forearms and backing her up to a wall. "Stop fighting me, okay. Just stop!"

"Let go of me," Emily said, trying her best to free herself from the grasp of his strong hands.

"Emily," Dante said in his efforts to calm her down. She was persistently trying to free herself from him and he fought to control her wild movements. "Emily!"

"Let me go! What's wrong with you?" she shouted. "Let me go!"

He listened this time, and unlatched his fingers from around her wrists.

"You're such a jerk...you freakin' animal!" She rubbed her wrists and said, "I have to find thirty-thousand dollars so I can get out of here. I can't take another minute anywhere near you! Ugh!" She headed back for the door, then took the elevators down to the ground floor, still rubbing her arms.

Venturing away from the resort, she stumbled into a bar, sat down and covered her face with her hands, trying to get herself together.

"You look like you can use several drinks," the bartender told her.

Emily looked up and saw a woman there, an African-American woman who appeared to have been in her late twenties. She was thin, had her hair pulled back into a ponytail.

Drawing in a breath, Emily said, "Yes. I can use several drinks, but I'll start off with one. What's popular around here?"

"I make a mean Bahama Mama."

"All right then. A mean Bahama Mama it is."

Emily rested her head against her arms. She needed to come up with a plan to get away from Dante and off of Pleasure Island. She sure wasn't getting any pleasure by being here, and she couldn't endure another night with Dante even if her life depended on it.

"Here you go, madam," the bartender said.

"Thank you."

"You're welcome."

Emily took a sip. "Mmm...this is good."

"Yeah, I put a little extra rum in there for ya."

"Thanks."

"So where are you visiting from?"

"Asheville, North Carolina."

"Oh...the mountains."

"Yes."

"What brings you to Pleasure Island? Vacationing?"

"Something like that. I sort of got married this weekend in the mass wedding at the GHC Resort."

"Cool," she said, her eyes lighting up. "I saw that on the news."

"Yeah, well I was one of the brides."

"And where's hubby?"

Emily shrugged. "I don't know. Probably back at the hotel, thinking up more ways to irritate me."

The bartender grinned.

Emily did too.

"I heard the owner of that place got hitched," the bartender said. "Is that true?"

"Um...what's his name?" Emily asked, playing along as if she wasn't aware who the owner was.

"Dante Champion. He's pretty popular around these parks."

Yeah, I bet, Emily thought.

The bartender continued, "His resort has helped a lot of people, you know. I sent my mom there after my dad died."

"Really?"

"Yep. She just needed the therapy aspect of it. She stayed for two weeks, thanks partially to a grant she received from Mr. Champion's GHC Foundation, and now, she's doing so much better."

Emily took another sip of her drink. "That's good."

"Yeah. It's amazing how he used a tragedy in his own life to focus on helping others."

Hiding a frown, Emily said, "Tragedy in his own life..."

"Yes. Girl, when I heard the story about what had happened to Mr. Champion, tears came to my eyes because, he's such an astute businessman. He carries himself very well. Very professional. Then I found out his wife died of cancer. She'd fought it for two years and he traveled the country, seeking different opinions, looking for a doctor who could save her, but there was nothing no one could do."

"Oh my gosh. That's terrible," Emily said, feeling sick to her stomach. She'd had Dante all wrong. He *had* known the pain of losing someone. He'd lost his wife. When he chatted with her online, as Armand, he told her that his wife had passed. He didn't say how she died, because he didn't like talking about it, but he *did* tell her and he was being truthful.

Emily couldn't believe she'd been so rude to him. She'd jumped to conclusions about Dante, assuming that he made up the story about his deceased wife in order to get close to her online but he had not made it up. He even used his tragedy to help others.

Emily turned up her drink to her mouth and took huge gulps.

"You want another?" the bartender asked, smiling.

"No. I have to go." She took out a twenty-dollar bill, placed it on the bar and said, "Thank you," then walked away.

Taking her phone from her purse, she called Melanie, listening to several rings before she heard, "Hey, Mrs. Champion!"

Emily shook her head. "Hey, Mel," she responded in a melancholy mood.

"Is everything okay?"

"No, not really."

"What's going on?"

"Well, I think I may have put my foot in my mouth."

"Uh oh. What have you done, Em?"

"Okay, so Dante and I were arguing earlier because I didn't join him for breakfast this morning or the marriage workshop. He told me that we could help each other, but I snapped...told him he didn't know what I was going through after losing Melvin, but turns out, he knows exactly what I'm going through. He was married before...lost his wife to cancer."

"Oh my gosh. I didn't know that."

"Exactly. And this entire time, I'm thinking he's just an arrogant pig, looking for the next woman to sleep with when, the reality is, he's the complete opposite. I truly believe he feels that we can help each other and all this time I've been so mean to him."

"Well, the least you can do is apologize."

"Yeah. I know."

"And then, cut the man some slack, Emily. Who knows? You just might learn to like him."

Emily sighed heavily. "Yeah, you're right. I'm going to go look for him."

"All right girl. Bye."

"Bye."

Emily began her walk back to the resort, pondering how she would approach Dante for an apology. But what if he wasn't receptive? What if he'd had enough of her? What if he'd given up and left the resort altogether?

When she walked in the suite, it was quiet and dark. Her first thought was that Dante had fallen asleep but he wasn't on the couch. She continued on to the bedroom and he wasn't there either. Then she peeped out onto the balcony. He wasn't there.

Back into the living room, she noticed his bags were still there. Maybe he'd gone to get a drink as she'd done. Deciding to just wait until he returned instead of going to look for him, she walked back into the bedroom, undressed then took a shower, thinking about how bitter she'd become in the two years she'd been without Melvin. Had his death really changed her so much to the point that being in the presence of any other man disgusted her – made her see all men as unworthy because the one man she wanted, the one she thought she would spend an eternity with had died in an automobile accident on his way home from work.

She remembered the day of the accident like it was yesterday...she'd been at home, looking over a business plan for the boutique when she received the phone call. Melvin had been in a terrible accident and was rushed to the nearest hospital.

She dropped everything and sped there, praying the whole way. Her breath almost escaped her several times as she tried to keep up with the thunderous beats of her heart.

At the hospital, she rushed in, frantically looking for a nurse or a doctor – someone who could tell her about an accident victim named Melvin Mitchell who'd just been brought in, introducing herself as his wife.

The look on the nurses' faces said it all. Then a doctor stepped out and said, "I'm sorry, Mrs. Mitchell. We did everything we could. His injuries were too severe and he lost a lot of blood."

Standing under the streams of water, she cried thinking about this. Maybe if she listened to Dante and kept an open mind about the resort by taking full advantage of the services they offered for those dealing with loss, it would help her to finally cope with Melvin's death and give her the courage to move on with her life.

Chapter 18

~ * ~

When Emily got up in the morning, Dante wasn't there. He'd been there because she could smell soap and cologne like he'd just taken a shower and headed out. She glanced at the clock. The time was 8:30 a.m. He was probably at breakfast.

She rushed to get ready. She wanted to join him this morning, especially since she didn't get a chance to talk to him last night. So after applying some makeup and brushing her hair, she took the elevator down to the ground floor and rushing to the restaurant, she saw Dante sitting alone. All the other men were sitting with their wives.

She walked over to his table, took a seat across from him, watching him glance up at her then back to his plate.

"Good morning," she said.

"Good morning," he responded, unenthused, still eating. Still looking down at his plate.

There was no smirk on his face, no sneaky look or suppressed smile, she noticed. He was quiet and disinterested.

Emily inhaled a deep breath and said, "I'm sorry."

That got his attention. He looked up at her confused. After he wiped his mouth with a napkin, he said, "Pardon me."

"I said, I'm sorry. I shouldn't have said those things

to you last night and I'm sorry for being difficult this entire week. I'm not usually like this."

He cracked a lazy, half smile and with raised eyebrows, he asked, "You're not?"

"No. Now does the smile mean you accept my apology?"

"Is that what you want it to mean?"

"That's what I hope it means."

"Then, yes, I accept your apology. And I'm sorry for grabbing your arms the way I did. If I hurt you—"

"I'm okay."

"You forgive me?"

"Yes, and I'll try not to be angry and bitter for the rest of this trip and make a real effort to enjoy the remainder of this journey."

"Let's shake on it," he suggested, to seal the deal and so that he could touch her hand in the process.

Emily extended her hand across the table to him for a shake.

He took her hand into his grasp, and said, "Are you certain you want to do this because I need you to be all in."

Emily felt a flame light up inside of her. "I'm sure."

"Good." He released her hand then took a sip of water while studying her for a moment. She appeared nervous, he noticed. "Have you eaten?" he asked.

"No."

"Well, there's a buffet with a variety of breakfast foods. Would you like for me to make you a plate?"

"I'll get it," she said, standing. "Besides, you don't know what I like."

"I think I would do a pretty good job of it."

She smiled and continued to the buffet of foods. Dante watched her as she walked, paying particular attention to her curvy backside. She had a nice body, something he noticed when he'd first laid eyes on her, but now that she was being rational and not the cranky, spastic woman she'd been for the last few days, he could enjoy just looking at her walk – the way her hips swayed from one side to the other.

* * *

After breakfast, they attended group couples counseling. In attendance were five other couples, sitting in chairs that circled the therapist who'd just finished outlining the stages of grief: denial, anger, bargaining, depression and acceptance. She said, of all of these stages, acceptance was the hardest because it was difficult to face the reality of never seeing someone that you loved and cared for again. Then she opened up the floor for people to share their story.

Emily looked around to see if anyone was going to voluntarily stand up and share their experience. No one moved. The room was eerily quiet. Dante was sitting to the right of her and out of her peripheral, she could see him staring at her. Had he even blinked?

Audrey, the woman she'd met at her boutique, stood up and decided to relate her story, and as everyone listened keenly, Emily could feel Dante's eyes on her again.

Dante had been examining her and he didn't care if she was aware of it or not. This was the first time he was this close to her and she didn't seem to mind it. He had a good view of her full, ripe lips and could smell her perfume, lotion or whatever she was wearing.

Emily swallowed hard when Dante leaned close to her. She could his body heat co-mingling with hers.

Whispering in her ear, he asked, "Are you going to share your story?"

Emily turned to look at him. He was only a few inches away from her face. This close up, she could see his distinctive features. He was clean-shaven, his face so smooth, she wanted to touch him there. The mustache above his lips enhanced them, made them full and enticing, so much so that she began to think about what they might feel like pressed against hers. The gentle look in his bright, hazel eyes let her know that he really wanted her to participate.

Holding his gaze, she whispered back, "I don't want to."

His eyes brightened when he watched her lips move. Had he even heard her?

"Dante, did you hear me?"

The way his name rolled off of her lips had left him somewhat speechless. He loved the way she pronounced it and he looked forward to hearing her say it more often, maybe even more frequently following heavy breathing, panting, and screams of *oohs* and *ahs*.

"Dante?" she said when she noticed he looked like he'd drifted off into a reverie.

"Yes. I heard you. We'll talk about it later."

* * *

"I'm surprised there wasn't an activity planned for today," Emily said as she sat across from Dante at another onsite restaurant where he'd taken her for dinner.

"There's not an activity planned for tomorrow either. It's time that couples are supposed to use to get to know each other."

"Oh. I see."

He took a sip of Bourbon and leaned back in his chair, staring at her as she finished up her meal. She'd changed into a royal blue dress that accentuated her skin tone and her curves. He examined her, every bite, every chew – the movement of her lips was a thing of beauty.

And her oval, dark brown eyes were ones he could gaze upon continuously. He'd dated beautiful women. Anita was a beautiful woman. But something about Emily Mitchell set his soul ablaze every time their eyes connected, when she brushed up against him, smiled at him or touched his hand.

"What?" she asked, her lips forming into a smile.

"Nothing."

"Why are you staring at me?"

"Just waiting for you to finish your meal so we can talk."

"I can talk and eat."

"I know. I'm just trying to be polite."

"Okay." Emily wiped her mouth. "I'm done. Now what's on your mind?"

"The things you told me online about your marriage to Melvin...were they true?"

"Yes."

"So you haven't been with a man since he died?"

Emily shook her head. "No."

"Why not?"

She shrugged. "I never had the desire to date or be around another man."

"Well that explains a lot," he said and flashed the most brilliant smile Emily had ever seen.

Emily grinned. "I just never, really recovered from his death and I don't think I ever will."

"See, that's why you need to be attending these therapy sessions. You heard what the doctor said this morning. Acceptance is the most difficult stage of grief."

"I think I have accepted it. I'm just not over it."

"Then you haven't accepted it, dear."

"Okay. Maybe not." Emily took a sip of water. "Can I ask you something?"

"Sure."

"Why didn't you tell me your wife passed?"

"I did tell you. It was one of the first things we discussed online, remember. You just chose to believe it was a lie once you found out that I was really Armand."

"How'd she die?"

He clenched his jaw. "She had breast cancer."

"Oh. You never told me that...online, I mean."

"I know. It's not something that I like to talk openly about." He took another sip of Bourbon. "I think my acceptance in the grieving process came even before she died."

"How so?"

"Well, once we found out she had cancer, we went to see all of these specialists and they were telling us the same thing – that there was nothing they could do. They only offered chemotherapy as an option to prolong her life. It worked for two years and during those years, I accepted the fact that she was going to die and there was nothing I could do about it. When she finally did pass, it hurt. It's been six years and I still miss her. I don't think that ever goes away."

"No it doesn't."

"I'll admit, the first three years were the hardest. The mutual friends we had all seemed to wither away. All I had was my brothers."

"So you're close with them?"

"Yeah. They're each in charge of running different departments within the company. I talked them into moving to Asheville and promised them I would singlehandedly make sure the company was a success and—"

"You did it."

He smiled. "How do you know?"

"I read an article about you in the paper."

His smile widened. "Really? So you've been reading up on me?"

"Well my girlfriend pretty much *made* me read it.

She's a huge fan of yours."

"Which girlfriend is that, so I can thank her?"

Emily laughed. "My friend Melanie. You had a business function at the hotel she works at about a week ago."

"And how do you know that?"

"She told me."

Dante smiled. "I remember her. She was very helpful."

"Melanie is a very good friend of mine."

"I know."

"And how do you know that?" she asked him.

"I have my ways." Dante took a sip of Bourbon. "So no man after Melvin?"

"No. How many women have you been with after Anita?"

"Wow."

"What?"

"The way you ask the question suggests that I've been with a ton of women after Anita."

"Then enlighten me."

"Okay. I dated maybe...um...twelve women. And before you ask, no, I did not sleep with all of them, and it was over the span of a few years. I was going through a stage in my life where I felt lonely and miserable all the time and I tried to fill that void with women. Then I realized what I was doing and how reckless I'd become so I changed that behavior...haven't been with a woman in three years."

"Three years. That's a long time for a man."

"And two years is a long time for a woman."

"No it's not. Women can hold out longer. We're looking for true love and romance."

"As am I. Hopefully now that we're married, I've finally found what I've been desiring for the last three years."

"I'm curious about something," Emily said. "Exactly why did you go through all of this just to end up with me?"

"You don't listen much, do you?" he asked with a smirk on his face.

"I do listen."

"No, because if you were, you would already know the answer because I told you why."

"Well, tell me again."

"Because I want you, and before you read too much into this, me wanting you has nothing to do with sex. With that being said, I would like very much to make love to my wife, but since that's not something you want, I'll try to be on my best behavior." A sly smile came to his lips. He knew he could seduce her at any time and any place, but what he wanted even more than that was for her to want him just as equally.

"There's something I've been meaning to ask you," she said.

"Shoot."

"What did you do with all those necklaces you bought from my boutique?"

He laughed. "I donated them to a women's shelter."

"And I thought you were giving them to your niece..."

"Yeah...I don't have a niece...I sort of made that part up just to have an excuse to make your acquaintance."

Emily blushed. "I figured as much."

"Did you?"

She nodded. "Yep. That's sweet of you, though...to donate those necklaces."

"Wow. My first compliment from Emily...hope it won't be my last."

She held his gaze, then looked away. There was something about the heat in his eyes that made her insides weak. Maybe she had missed being with a man moreso than she thought...more than she would admit to. Dante was oozing sex appeal out of his pores. He was extremely good-looking and could definitely get any woman he desired.

"Let's take a walk," he suggested.

"Okay."

They strolled along the beach at night. There were a lot of people out, no doubt enjoying the nightlife in such a beautiful place.

"So where is your family?" Dante asked, walking side-by-side with her watching the light breeze blow her hair away from her ear.

"My parents live in Jacksonville, Florida."

"Retired?"

"Yes. They retired there. My mother was a school teacher and my father worked for the postal service."

"I noticed, when we were messaging each other, you didn't mention them much."

"That's because I don't talk to them as much as I used to."

"Why not?"

"Um..." Emily sighed. "It's just that every single time I call them, they ask me how I'm coping and if I need to see a therapist."

Dante nodded. He could understand why they would ask the question, especially after the loss she had experienced.

Emily interrupted his thoughts and said, "After getting that out of the way, then comes the dialogue about when I'm going to get married again and have some babies."

"Wow."

"Exactly. Now you see why I don't talk to them a lot."

"Well, to be honest, my parents were the same way

when Anita died. They were always on my back about remarrying. My mother used to tell me that I needed someone to cook for me...told me I was getting skinny and needed some meat on my bones."

Emily smiled and looked him up and down inconspicuously. He wasn't skinny in her book. Skinny men were just that – straight up and down flimsy with no muscle definition. Dante was more of the athletic type and everywhere her eyes roamed on his body, she could see muscle definition from the firm ropes in his calves to the lightning bolts in his neck, forearms and biceps.

"The real reason she wanted me to marry was because, since I'm the oldest, she said my brothers looked up to me and, therefore, they would do what I did."

"You believe that?"

"To a certain degree, but my brothers are their own men, and being such, they make their own decisions."

Emily nodded in agreement.

"Anyway, back to my parents...my father died three years after Anita and a year after he died, my mother passed away."

"Oh my gosh. I'm so sorry to hear that. I know it must've been rough on you and your brothers."

"It was, but we got through. Now the reason I told you that is to tell you this...enjoy your parents while you have them, sweetie, because they will not be around forever."

"You're right. I need to call them soon."

Dante stopped walking and turned to face Emily, just staring down at her face. At her lips. "You want to sit for a while."

"Sure."

Emily sat down with her legs folded in Indian-style, facing the ocean.

Dante sat down in front of her, blocking her view of

the water.

Emily didn't mind it. She'd much rather look at him than trying to strain her eyes to see the ocean at nighttime. Just the tranquil sound of the wrestling water was enough for now.

Dante stared at her for a moment, catching her gaze a few times before she would quickly look away. The woman he'd fallen in love with online was here and he planned on taking advantage of the time he had to get to know her one-on-one like this, as he had online.

"You're shy," he said.

"Is that a question or a statement?" she asked, all smiles.

"It's an observation."

"How do you figure?"

"Well, for one thing, you can't hold eye contact for longer than a few seconds."

"I can, just not with you."

"Oh, really?" he asked, smiling, then seductively biting his bottom lip. "Why's that?"

She shrugged, not wanting to give him an explanation. How do you tell a man that he's so fine, he blew your mind in every way possible...so freakin' good-looking that you had to look away to catch your breath?

"Come on. See, that's what I'm talking about. You give me a timid shrug and that's all I get?"

"I'm just not used to being open and conversational with anyone besides Melvin. It's like, I knew him. I knew what he liked, what he didn't like. I was extremely comfortable with him, and I knew that he had my back no matter what. That if it came down to my life or his, he'd die for me in a heartbeat."

So would I. It was on the tip of his tongue and on his mind, but Dante held in his thoughts so she could continue confiding in him. Melvin meant a lot to her. He could understand that better than anyone, having dealt with the loss of his wife.

Emily raked her hands in the sand, gathering some of it together rubbing it in her hands and brushing it off.

"I think that, if you share your story in group therapy, it will help you tremendously."

Emily shook her head. "I can't."

"Why not?"

"Because when I talk about Melvin too much I cry and I can't stop crying."

"This will help you with that. You may not think so initially, but after you've shared your story, you'll see what I mean."

Emily batted her eyes to fight tears away.

"Look at me, Emily," he requested in a soft, concerned voice, taking her hands into his.

When she did, a lone tear rolled from her eye and down her face. "I'm going to go," she said. Removing her hands from his grasp, she stood up.

"Emily."

"I'm sorry, Dante. I'm just going to take a shower and go to bed," she said and rushed off.

Dante blew an agitated breath. He hated to have upset her when he only wanted her to talk about her feelings. She needed to let Melvin go so she could make room in her heart for him.

Chapter 19

~ * ~

Emily took a quick five-minute shower then moisturized her body in a raspberry lotion before sliding into a silk, white gown. She stepped out of the bathroom and slid under the covers into bed, lying there, thinking about Melvin. She hadn't accepted the fact that Melvin was gone and wasn't coming back. That's why she couldn't stand up in group and tell her story. She was still pretending it hadn't happened, still grieving. Then she thought about what grief was – keen mental suffering or distress over a loss. Were there rules about how long a person was supposed to grieve? How long was too long? Could grief over the death of a loved one ever be conquered? If so, was this grief retreat really the way to do it?

She inhaled a much needed breath as tears ran down her face, towards her ears before wetting her pillow.

The knock at the door jolted her, but she hadn't responded to see what Dante wanted.

"Emily, are you sleeping?" Dante waited a moment for an answer, but when he hadn't heard anything, he turned the knob, walked in and saw her lying on the bed – a white sheet covering her body. He walked closer to the bed. Her eyes were opened. He stooped down and said, "I didn't mean to upset you, Emily."

Emily saw a blurred version of him through her tears. "Everything you said about me is right," she told him. "I haven't accepted the fact that Melvin is gone. I don't know how...how do I move on without him?" she cried.

The sound of her whimpering and the way sadness distorted her voice touched him deeply. It hurt him...felt like a knife was being driven through his heart. All he wanted was to make everything right for her but he couldn't do that when most of her problem was an internal one – not one that money could fix. "Sweetheart, that's why we're here, and if you trust me, I'll help you. I give you my word, Emily." He reached for her hand. "Will you trust me?"

She sniffled and wiped her eyes. "Yes," she responded, accepting his hand.

Dante scooped her up into his arms. He used his index finger to trace and wipe away the tears that fell from her eyes. "Please stop crying."

"I will eventually, when I fall asleep," she said sadly. "Will you lie here with me for a while?"

"Of course, dear."

And he did. After wishing her a good night, he watched her close her eyes. She was a broken soul and he'd planned on fixing her again.

When he knew she was sleeping, he left a kiss on her temple, tucked her carefully into bed and, like a gentleman, he headed for the couch where he rested, thinking about her.

Chapter 20

~ * ~

Over breakfast, Dante mentioned to Emily that he was going to share his story today at group therapy. He hadn't planned on it, but in order to motivate her to talk openly about Melvin's death, he wanted her to see him do the same about Anita.

So, during therapy, he'd stood up and boldly told his story about how Anita had battled cancer for two years until her body couldn't take anymore. Until she was too tired, too drained, too sick to fight any longer. After he was done, he sat down, leaned over in her ear and whispered, "Go ahead. I'm here for you, sweetie."

Again, Emily told him she wasn't ready, but if she wasn't ready now, especially after hearing him tell his story, when would she ever be ready?

Dante tried to talk her into it again, but she adamantly refused. His patience was wearing thin. He tried to suppress his frustration by taking a deep breath but he was unsuccessful. Anyone looking at him could see he was upset. But still, he sucked it all in and told himself that he'd coach her through this, but before he could give her further encouragement, she stood up and walked away.

She was giving up, quitting, and he hated that. He wasn't a quitter and he certainly didn't want one for a spouse. But molding her into the woman he wanted her to be was proving to be more than he bargained for. He rubbed his hands over his eyes and stood up, going on a hunt to find her and fast before he lost the nerve to do what he was about to do. It was a new day and she was wasting it.

Not anymore.

When he stepped in the suite, he walked to the bedroom where he knew she would be, and there she was, sitting there brooding on the edge of the bed with her arms crossed underneath her breasts.

He stood in the doorway, leaned up against the frame with his arms crossed, watching her for a few moments as he juggled all kind of thoughts twirling around in his head. He didn't want to be too firm on her, but he had to do something drastic so she knew he meant business.

"How is this supposed to work, Emily, when you refuse make an attempt to try?"

"I *am* trying," she shot back.

"How? How are you trying when every time I tell you to participate in group, you refuse to take part in the program."

"I just need time."

"Time?"

"Yes. Time. I can't do everything on your timeframe, Dante. I know you want me to magically forget about Melvin overnight—"

"No. That's not what I want."

"Then what *do* you want?"

"Why ask me what *I* want when your actions have proven you don't care?"

Emily shook her head. She'd already had a headache and she hated feeling pressured like this by Dante. "Dante, please. My life is already messed up enough to go back and forth with you over a bunch of nonsense."

"Nonsense? Getting your life together is nonsense?"

"Listen. I'm fine. I—"

"Yeah. Keep telling yourself that. Maybe one day you'll believe it."

"I already do believe it. I certainly don't need you telling me otherwise, like you know me."

"I do know you!" he snapped. "I spent three months of my life knowing you, Emily. I don't know every single detail of your life history, but what I *do* know is you're living in denial and until you make some changes, you're going to continue being miserable and lonely."

"I'm not mis—"

"And don't tell me you're not miserable because I see it every time I look into your eyes. All I wanted you to do was give this trip your all, but you refuse to participate, just like you refuse to wear the ring I hand picked for you...it's been on the nightstand since the ceremony last Saturday. And just to think I used to pride myself on having the acute ability to read people, but I failed with you because I thought you had feelings for me, but I see now that I was horribly mistaken. So you're free to go. I'll pay the breach of contract penalty on your behalf. All you have to do is pack your bags and run back home to your canned world of false hopes and dwindling memories of a man who can't love you anymore because he's incapable of doing such."

Dante walked away from the door and soon after, Emily heard him leave the suite.

Tears poured down her face at the realization that she'd lost a good man in Melvin, but he was gone, and now, she was on the verge of losing another good man, a living, breathing, passionate one who'd just angrily dismissed himself from her presence.

Chapter 21

~ * ~

Dante sat at a table out by the pool, trying to cool off. He was on the phone with his brother Dimitrius; a pair of Cartier sunglasses masking his worried eyes – worried that he was about to lose the woman he'd waited so long for.

"You told her to leave? The woman you've been practically stalking for the last six months?" Dimitrius asked. Dimitrius was the level-headed brother, the one Dante could talk to about anything. The one who could offer some good advice.

He drew in a breath and said, "Yeah, man. I did. I told her to go."

"Why would you do something like that?"

"She just doesn't get it. She prefers to sulk in self pity and pretend she's fine when I can clearly see she's not, so I did what was best for her and told her to go."

"You sound like you're pretty bummed about it."

"I am. A part of me wants to run back up there to the suite and stop her from packing her bags because I know that's what she's doing, especially since I gave her an out. Then another part of me wants her to go. I've never had to chase a woman before. And after all I've done – joining the GHC site just to get a chance to talk to her, visiting her store and buying out inventory just to be near her for five minutes, she's still not giving me what I want."

"And what's that?"

"I want her to acknowledge the fact that we're married and stop treating this like a joke. I want her to let the therapists we have at this resort help her overcome her grief...help her move on from Melvin so she can see me for the man I am. But every time I try to get her to take a step forward in the right direction, she takes three steps back and I just can't keep getting my hopes up, trying to convince myself she'll come around and she never does."

"That's tough, bro, but I have to say I think you've done the right thing here. You gave her the option to leave. Now the ball is in her court, and I know you would prefer to be an active participant in this process for her, but it's your turn to be a spectator. I know that's difficult for you, Mr. C.E.O., but you have to sit back, relax and let her make the next move. Then you'll know how to move forward."

"And what if she leaves?" Dante said rubbing his hand across his head, frustrated. "I really don't want her to leave, even though I told her to go."

"Dang, bro. This girl really got you going...sounds to me like you might've fallen hard for Ms. Emily."

Dimitrius was right. He had fallen hard for Emily.

"Do you love her?" Dimitrius asked.

"Yes. I love her. I love everything about her except for the unhealthy fixation she has with her deceased husband."

"It *must* be love. I've never seen you so intent on getting a woman."

Dante sighed.

"Unfortunately, though, you may have to let her go," Dimitrius advised.

Dante frowned. It wasn't something he wanted to hear, but he knew Dimitrius would tell you straight up whether you wanted to hear it or not.

"I understand that," Dante said, "Even though I can't accept it. I won't accept it."

"Then you know what you have to do, right? You have to tell her how you feel, Dante. Tell her you love her, that you want this marriage to work and you'll do everything in your power to *make* it work."

Dante nodded.

* * *

Dante had been nervous about going back up to the suite. If her suitcase was missing, then he was certain she was on her way back home.

When he arrived, he saw her suitcase on the bed. Some clothes were in it, neatly folded. Another small pile of clothes were lying on the bed next to the suitcase. She'd certainly been packing, but she wasn't there at the moment.

* * *

"And where's Mr. Champion, Emily?" the therapist asked. "We need both parties in our group sessions."

Emily had ventured down to the last group therapy session of the evening. In the midst of packing her bags and leaving, she got the urge to do what Dante had been pestering her to do for days now – share her story. So instead of leaving the resort and going home, she headed downstairs to do just that.

Emily stood up and said, "I don't know where he is, but I've never participated in group and I want to this evening. I need to."

"Okay, then. Go right ahead."

"Um," Emily began, her hands balled into fists as she tried to ease her nervousness. Her eyes filled with tears and her heart was being hammered with ferocious beats. "Um..."

"Just take your time, Emily. We're all friends here."

"Okay...um...I was married to a wonderful man named Melvin Mitchell. He was the light of my life...the love of my life and he died in a car accident two years ago. I thought..." she said, and her voice cracked. "I thought that if I ignored what I felt, the pain would go away but it hasn't." Her lips trembled as she tried to get her thoughts together.

"Take your time, Emily," the therapist said, watching Emily struggle.

"I...I remember getting the phone call like the accident just happened yesterday. I was at home and I sped to the hospital, trying to get there as fast...as...I...could, but," her lips trembled. "But I..." she said, struggling to find her breath. "I didn't...make it." She breathed in and out rapidly and suddenly the room was spinning and then she fainted, hitting her head on a chair before she landed on the floor.

Chapter 22

~ * ~

Dante headed down to the ground floor again, hoping he'd find Emily and convince her to stay. When he arrived in the lobby, however, he saw a crowd that had gathered. A few women were crying and there was a fire truck parked in the emergency lane in front of the hotel.

"What's going on?" he asked the first person he came upon, one of the cleaning staff members.

"I think somebody passed out or something," the man said. "That's what everybody else is saying."

Dante continued on through the crowd. This was his resort and he needed to know what was going on right now. He saw Dr. Stacey, one of the therapists, outside with her hands crossed, so he pushed the glass door open and said, "What's going on here?"

"Oh my gosh, Mr. Champion," Dr. Stacey said, her hands trembling. "She fainted and hit her head."

Dante frowned. "Who fainted?"

"Emily."

The frown deepened in his forehead and for a moment his heart stopped. "My Emily?"

"Yes. She was trying to share with the group and she just blacked out."

For a moment, Dante felt like *he* was going to faint. Had he heard Dr. Stacey correctly? Emily fainted? He gathered himself enough to get his head on straight and had one of his resort drivers escort him to the hospital as quickly as he could.

Once he arrived, he rushed in the emergency room entrance, and summoning the first nurse he saw, he asked, "Where's the woman that just came in? Emily Champion? Where is she?"

"Sir, she's being checked out by a doctor at the moment."

"I need to see her," he said desperately, feeling like his heart was about to jump out of his chest.

"Sir, if you would just calm down a moment—"

"No. I need to see my wife, now! Where is she?" When the nurse hadn't responded, he looked at the double gray doors behind her and walking past the nurse, ignoring her calls to come back and sit the waiting area, he continued on, pushing the doors open and walking the emergency room corridor, frantically searching for Emily. Straight ahead he saw her, sitting on the edge of a bed with a few band-aids at her temple.

Hearing nothing but the beats of his own heart, he ran to her as fast as he could.

Emily didn't realize he was there until the seconds before he wrapped his arms around her, pressing the side of her face against his chest. While he held her there, she could feel his rapid, uncontrolled heartbeats pounding against her face.

"I'm sorry, baby. I'm so sorry," he said, taking full responsibility. He was the one who'd pushed her to relay her story to the group, even when she told him she wasn't ready to do so.

"I'm okay, Dante."

"I'm sorry," he said again, his arms still wrapped around her, holding her tightly.

"I'm okay."

He released her so he could see her face. He held her head between his hands, pressed his lips against hers and, after taking a kiss, he asked, "Are you okay, baby? Please tell me you're okay."

"I'm okay," she said, staring longingly into his worried eyes.

"She had what we would call an anxiety attack," the doctor told him. "In addition to that, she's dehydrated. We're going to give her a few IV drips overnight while we observe her and she may be ready to be discharged early in the A.M."

"Why does she have the band-aids on her temple?"

"From what I gather, when she fell, she bumped her head. We've already given her a CT scan and there's no internal damage there...just the cut. We gave her a few stitches."

Dante swallowed hard.

"If you would step out in the hallway for a moment, Sir, we can get her set up," the doctor said.

"No. I'm staying here. I'll move in a corner so I'm out of your way, but I'm staying here with my wife."

"All right, Sir."

And he did just what he said. Dante stood in the corner, while the nurses prepped Emily in the hospital bed, connecting an IV to her and making sure she was comfortable with enough blankets to keep her warm in the cool environment.

When the nurses left the room, Dante sat in the chair next to her bed, his eyes fixed on her so firmly, he hadn't blinked.

"Dante."

"Yes, sweetie."

"I passed out, but I did it. I got a good chunk of the story out before I fainted."

"You don't have to talk about that, Emily."

"No, I want to. I took your advice, told my story and I feel better."

"Good," Dante said, but it didn't seem that she was

better. She was lying on a hospital bed, courtesy of him.

"I'm ready to fully participate now. We have four days left and I promise to make the most of every moment."

"Okay," he responded.

"You don't seem too excited about that."

"I'm not," he said truthfully.

"Why? I thought that's what you wanted."

"It is, but if I knew my pushing you to participate would have you ending up in a hospital bed, I would've never done it."

"But I'm fine, Dante."

"I'm relieved that you are, but—"

"Just let that be enough for right now," she said.

Dante nodded. "Okay."

Chapter 23

~ * ~

In the morning, Emily was discharged from the hospital. Dante took extra special care to make sure she was comfortable at the suite. He removed her suitcase from the bed and laid her there.

"Dante, I'm fine. You don't have to cater to me."

"I want to take care of you, Emily. Now you stay here and rest. I'm going to go get us some breakfast."

She smiled. "Okay."

When Dante left the suite, Emily called Sherita just to check in and to see how things were going at the boutique. Afterwards, she dialed Melanie.

"Are things getting better?" Melanie inquired.

"If you call passing out and having to go to the hospital to get stitches *better*, then yes."

"You passed out?"

"Yes."

"How did that happen?"

"Well, Dante was telling me how I wasn't participating...said something about me being miserable and lonely, and I don't want *miserable* and *lonely* to be words that describes me. So I sucked it up and went to group therapy to share my story about Melvin and I fainted."

"Oh...my...gosh!"

"Before I crashed and burned, I remember crying buckets and feeling lightheaded. Then I'm waking up with people huddled around me."

"Jeez, Em. Maybe you should just come home."

"Nope. I won't. I may have fell and hit my head, Melanie, but I think I had a breakthrough."

"How so?"

"Sharing my story with the group has opened my eyes. Dante was right. I *do* feel better after talking openly about Melvin. It feels like a weight has been lifted from my shoulders."

"That's good."

"Yes, and with four more days here in paradise, I'm going to enjoy myself."

"Well, good for you. You deserve to enjoy yourself. And maybe you can enjoy a little of Dante, too," Melanie quipped. "Oh, no, wait...my bad. I mean a *lot* of Dante."

Emily giggled. "Hey, Dante is coming back with breakfast in a few minutes, so I'm going to go."

"Okay, girl. Bye."

As she was placing her cell phone on the nightstand, she heard the latch at the door. Dante came walking into the bedroom with a breakfast tray, setting it on the bed.

"Hope I got enough."

Emily glanced at the tray. He'd gotten plenty of everything...eggs, hash browns, bacon, toast and slices of fresh cut oranges. She glanced up at him, watching his sexy lips curve into a smile. She smiled too. "Yeah. You got plenty."

"Good."

Emily took a fork full of eggs to her mouth and noticed Dante wasn't eating. Instead, he was looking at her and she could tell he had a lot on his mind. She continued eating, and he took his gaze from her to her suitcase that he'd placed by the door.

Dante rubbed his head.

Emily hadn't cared for his company much before, but having found out that he'd been right about her healing process, she began to notice how, whenever he was frustrated or worried about something, he would rub his head or look away from her. When he was nervous, and men *do* get nervous, he would lock his hands together and rest his chin on them, or if he was standing, he'd slide his hands in his pockets. And when he was angry, his eyes and face would darken and everything about him exuded irritation and frustration. He was the type that couldn't mask an angry demeanor.

At the moment, he looked to be worried. Emily was almost certain that he was. The man had the appetite of a lion and he hadn't taken a bite of anything on his plate.

"Dante."

"Yes?" he said, taking his eyes off of her suitcase and giving her his full attention.

"Why aren't you eating?"

"Lost my appetite when I thought something bad had happened to you."

"How many times do I have to tell you that I'm fine?"

"I know, baby. It's just that, walking those hospital hallways brought back so many bad memories of taking Anita to chemotherapy, watching her get worse and worse...hearing the noises from those machines..."

"I'm sorry."

"No, *I'm* sorry. If I hadn't yelled at you, you probably would not have been in there in the first place."

Emily didn't respond to him. Instead, she ate more, then stood up and said, "Be right back," rushing off to the bathroom.

After a few minutes, she came out and noticed Dante hadn't moved. He was still sitting on the bed, his head hanging low, like he was sad or in deep thought.

"So are you going to leave?" he asked without even

looking up at her.

In a bold move, she walked closer to him and when he knew she was getting closer, he looked up, watching her stand between his legs. "Do you want me to leave, Dante?" she asked, touching the sides of his face.

He frowned slightly, confused by her touch. She'd never touched him intentionally before. As a matter of fact, no woman had ever touched him like this since Anita. Emily's touch was tender, something he hadn't expected – something he didn't feel he deserved because he blamed himself for the bandage on her temple – for her having to go to the hospital.

Meeting her gaze, he responded truthfully, "No, I don't want you to go, but all I ever seem to do is hurt you, Emily, and I don't want to hurt you anymore."

"Then don't hurt me," she said softly, pressing her lips against his forehead.

Dante closed his eyes when he felt her warm lips against his skin, feeling desire rattle him to his core.

"I have a private therapy session with Dr. Stacey at ten," Emily said. "She told me I could bring you for support if I needed to, and I would like for you to come with me if that's okay."

"Are you sure?"

"Yes, Dante. I'm sure."

* * *

After the two-hour long therapy session, the two went to lunch together and when Dante asked her what they would do with the hours they had to burn before dinner, Emily had a suggestion.

She took him by the hand and led him to the docks.

"This is what you want to do?" Dante asked, surprised. "You want to get on a rowboat, because the last time you were so angry with me, I thought you were going to jump in the water and never resurface."

Emily laughed. "The last time was rough, I know, but I want to go again. I owe you."

Dante nodded. "Okay. Let's do it."

Dante checked out a boat, helped her onboard then stepped on himself. They both used the oars to row along quietly for a while, enjoying the weather.

"It's a beautiful day," she told him.

"Yes it is," he responded, staring at her from head to toe. She was beautiful, wearing a white sundress with her curly strands blowing in the wind, her eyes hiding behind a pair of dark shades.

When they were further along, she said, "I was wrong about you."

"How so?"

She shrugged. "I thought you were arrogant and egotistical."

He smirked. "That's what most people think about me. It comes with the success, especially for a man."

Emily nodded in agreement. "And I didn't think you were the least bit interested in me other than to have me in your bed once or twice."

"Has your opinion changed?"

She smiled and nodded, feeling the wind against her face, staring at the strong man sitting in front of her, using his upper body to row. He wore a gray T-shirt today and a pair of jean shorts. With every stroke of the oar, she could see his arm muscles bulge. Even the hair on his legs added to his overall manliness. Sexiness.

"Last night, when I was sitting on that hospital bed and I looked up and saw the panic in your eyes, my opinion changed."

"Changed how?" he asked and stopped rowing.

"I knew you actually cared about me. I could see the worry in your eyes."

"I *was* worried, and you're right. I do care about you, Emily. Very much."

Emily smiled, her hair blowing in her face.

Dante raked it away and then, he pulled her sunglasses from her eyes.

She squinted because of the brightness of the sun and said, "You take my sunglasses off, but you leave yours on? That's not fair..."

He pulled his shades from his face and said, "Is that better?"

"Yes, that's a lot better. Now I can see those gorgeous, hazel eyes of yours."

He leaned in close to her and when she hadn't resisted, he planted a soft kiss against her lips, tasting her in a more provocative way than he had in the hospital last night. When he pulled away from her, he noticed her eyes were still closed, the wind still blowing her hair in front of her face.

Then she opened her eyes, looked at him and smiled.

"What?" he asked.

"You, literally, almost took my breath away."

"You have no idea what I'm capable of doing to you, Emily," he said with arrogant eyes.

Emily smiled. She knew exactly what he meant and she knew he had the tools, the passion, and desire to do whatever he claimed he would. "Can I have my sunglasses back now?"

"Sure," he said, handing them to her.

She slid them back on his face, and he followed suit, sliding his sunglasses on as well.

"So how do you keep it all together? You have your multi-million dollar business, your personal life, then dealing with loss...how do you not choke under the pressure of it all."

"I give."

"Huh?"

"I give. A great man once said, there's more

happiness in giving than there is in receiving."

She nodded.

"So I give...I donate money to shelters, food banks, schools...I even formed a foundation that offers grants to help people who are suffering a loss to be able to afford therapy. Knowing that I'm helping others gives me satisfaction."

"That's very admirable. A lot of wealthy people don't give money to charities or anyone else for that matter. People tend to be greedy and stingy these days."

"You're right."

"I had a discussion with my friend Melanie not too long ago about how these famous people get on TV and ask the public for donations to help feed children who are living in poverty, but they have *way* more money than the general population...seems weird for a millionaire or billionaire to practically beg for money to help the poor when they are filthy rich and can help in ways that someone like myself can't. I don't get that."

The smile on his face had her curious.

"What?" she asked.

"I can't believe we're actually having a conversation and you're not trying to kill me."

Emily looked amused. "You know what I mean though, right? About the rich..."

"Yes. I get it, but I'll tell you why that's the case. See, these non-profit organizations seek famous people to do commercials because they know people can relate to this person. They're stars. Household names. People will be more apt to donate money if someone they feel like they *know* are the ones asking for it."

Emily nodded. "Yeah. I suppose that could be the case. My point is, they can skip the commercial altogether and give the organization a few million of their own money and call it a day."

"That's an interesting perspective."

Emily's cell phone rang, interrupting their flow.

"You brought your phone?" Dante asked with a smirk.

"Yes...just in case you tried something," she said, suppressing a smile while taking her phone from her small purse. "It's my friend, Sherita. She's running the boutique for me while I'm here."

"You need to take it?"

"No. I'll call her back later." Emily slid the phone back into her purse.

"Are you sure, because you can take it if you need to?"

"Nah. She just calls me to keep me up-to-date on the store. I'm sure everything's fine."

"Speaking of the store, how is everything going?"

"It's...ah...it's okay."

"That didn't sound convincing."

"Well, it could be better."

"How's that?"

"The boutique market is flooded...there are boutiques all around town. And it doesn't help that items in my store costs up to forty percent more than other stores."

"Hmm," he responded.

"And my store is pretty much outdated as you saw when you came there, I'm sure, but I'm not complaining. I like my little store. It keeps me busy and it pays the rent, so..."

Dante nodded. "There's nothing like getting paid for doing what you love, right."

"Right."

* * *

Later in the evening, they went to dinner, at a seafood restaurant that Dante had recommended, just on the outskirts of the resort. They'd arrived just in time because when they were settled at a table, the rain came down heavy, pounding against the window where they sat.

Dante was busy trying to convince Emily to try oysters for the first time.

"No thanks," she told him. "The last time somebody talked me into trying something I didn't like, I broke out in hives."

"Well, in that case, don't try it. I wouldn't want anything to happen to that pretty face of yours," he said, then slurped down another oyster. "Mmm...you don't know what you're missing, though."

"How many of those do you normally eat?"

"Not very many...the most I've eaten at a time were maybe around twenty or twenty-five."

"And you eat them raw?"

"That's the best way to eat it, baby," he said, sucking another one down in one huge slurp.

Emily smiled. He was eating those oysters so good, she was tempted to try one. "Okay, I'll do it," she said, feeling adventurous.

"Really? You want to try it?"

"Yeah."

He squeezed some fresh lemon juice on the oyster and added a little cocktail sauce. Then he picked up the shell and handed it to her. "Okay, so you can tilt the shell up to your mouth and slurp like I do, or you can use the oyster knife to sort of rake it out of the shell and into your mouth."

"I'll do what you do," she said, then braced herself. "Okay. Here goes." With the shell tilted to her mouth, she slurped the oyster from the shell, feeling the slithery sensation in her mouth.

"Chew for a few seconds, then swallow," he instructed her.

She did exactly what he said and after swallowing, she said, "Mmm...that was pretty good. I didn't know what to expect, but that wasn't bad. Not bad at all."

"I thought you might like it."

Emily wiped her mouth and took a sip of red wine. "I have to admit...I'm having a wonderful time with you, Dante."

"I'm having the time of my life with you, Emily."

Chapter 24

~ * ~

After dinner, they headed back for the hotel by way of the beach. Emily took off her sandals, holding them in her left hand, walking barefoot on the cool, wet night sand.

Dante grasped her right hand with his left and held on to it. He noticed that Emily didn't snatch her hand away from his, but instead, held on firmly to it in this romantic setting. And he felt something akin to current run through her hand to his. Maybe it was nerves, the same spark he felt when his lips had touched hers for the first time.

"What are you thinking about?" he asked her.

"All the work I have to do when I get home."

"No, no, no. You can't be thinking about work while you're here with me. I need your full attention."

Emily flashed a half smile and felt a few rain drops pelt her face. "Okay, we better run before we get drenched."

"That was just a few drops. We got time."

Just then, the rain picked up faster and the two scrambled for shelter, running hand-in-hand as fast as they could to the hotel.

"I told you we were going to get wet," Emily said laughing as they stood in the hotel lobby.

"Next time I'll listen to you, darling."

They continued on to the elevator, stepping onto it.

Dante pressed the eight button and when the doors closed, his eyes locked on Emily like an animal seeking its prey. She was standing in the back corner with her arms crossed, opposite of him, her wet hair dangling around her face. He imagined that they were at his home, in the shower together being drenched by the massive rain shower heads above. Her legs would be wrapped around his waist while he took her in a way that he'd never taken any other woman. Her nails in his back. His tongue down her throat.

"Did you hear me?" she asked him.

He snapped out of his trance. "You said something?"

"Yes. I said it's good to play in the rain sometimes," she said smiling.

You have no idea, is what he was thinking.

"Where were you just now?" she asked.

Lost in all of your beauty. "I'm here. I was just thinking about what you said. I haven't ran in the rain like that in a while. It's refreshing."

"It is, but now that we're inside in the air conditioning, I'm cold."

Dante could tell she was cold as indicated by her nipples poking through the wet blouse that clung to her breasts. When the elevator doors opened up to the eleventh floor, she said, "Well, now we can get out of these wet clothes."

Emily walked in the room and he followed. "I'm going to take a hot shower," she told him.

"Think I will, too," he responded. "In my shower of course." A sly grin appeared on his face.

Emily smiled, too.

While taking a shower, she thought about what he said at dinner, about how she should reach out to her mother because her mom had good intentions. She hadn't spoken to her parents in months, and she wanted nothing other than to talk to them now. But that call would have to wait for a decent hour. Surely they were in bed, sound asleep by now.

When she was done showering, she blow-dried her hair and applied lotion to her body – her usual nighttime routine. Then she stepped in the bedroom, ready to rest after having one of the best days of her life with Dante.

Lying on the bed, staring up at the ceiling, she couldn't sleep. All she could do was think about Dante, how she'd judged the man based on rumors she'd heard. Once she'd gotten to know him personally, anything everyone else had to say was irrelevant.

Emily sighed. She wanted to go into the living room where Dante had been sleeping. She felt a strange urge to be close to him, something that hadn't happened since Melvin, but she felt it with Dante. She wondered if it was because he was the only man she'd spent a considerable amount of time with since Melvin had passed. Or, maybe it was the fact that she'd had an amazing day with him, first in therapy, then on their boat ride and dinner, followed by a romantic stroll on the beach.

A few light taps at the door invaded her thoughts.

"Yes?"

"Just wanted to see if you were sleeping," Dante said through the closed door.

Emily smiled. Apparently, Dante couldn't sleep either. "Come in," she told him.

Dante turned the knob and entered the room, smelling the sweet fragrance of her lotion. The room was dimly lit with a little light coming from the bathroom. Emily had purposely left a crack in the bathroom door for that purpose.

"Hey," she said, watching him walk to the same side of the bed where he'd rested yesterday. Where he'd held her. The only difference was, he wasn't wearing a shirt this time and she could feel his body heat flirt with hers. The hair on his chest added to his manliness and his iron pecks made her want to touch him. "You can't sleep?"

"No, not really."

"Good. You can keep me company for a while. Can you rest here next to me, like you did last night?"

"Yeah," he said, standing up to move the covers back, then slid under and laid down facing her. "You smell delicious."

Emily chuckled. "Thanks."

"You're welcome."

After a few moments of silence, she said, "You're a mystery, Dante."

"How's that?"

"You haven't had a real relationship in years, yet, you go through all of this trouble to be with me."

"What trouble?" he asked, displaying a smile that could cause a woman's heart to stop.

"You know what I mean. Before you came in, I was lying here thinking about that."

"Oh, now the truth comes out. You *do* think about me."

She giggled. "Well, we had such a good day today that I couldn't help but think about you."

"It's all good, sweetie. I was thinking about you too."

"You were?"

"Yes, but then again, I'm always thinking about you," he drawled out smoothly and seductively. When she sighed, he knew he was wearing her down, forcing her to let down her walls.

"Do you have children?" she asked to change the subject a little while abating the sexual tension in the room.

"Wow. That's out of left field."

"I was just thinking about some things I don't know about you and that's one of them."

"No, I don't have children," he said, reaching to rake her curls away from her face with the tips of his fingers again.

She closed her eyes and nearly lost all of her senses when she felt his warm fingers against her face. "Do you want children?" she managed to ask.

"Yes. I want children. I want them with you, Emily," he said honestly.

Emily's heart melted. She found his left hand with her right and threaded their fingers together.

Dante closed his eyes at the feel of her soft hand, thinking about how other parts of her body must feel if her hands were this soft.

Chapter 25

~ * ~

In the morning, Emily woke up to somewhat of a surprise. Instead of her head resting on her pillow, she was lying on Dante's warm, firm chest. His arms were wrapped around her and she could feel his hands on her back, underneath her night shirt.

She sat up slowly and looked at him. She didn't recall anything happening between them last night other than talking, but why was she resting against his chest?

Dante saw the puzzled look on her face and said, "Good morning, sweetie."

"Good morning. Um...how did I get in this position?"

"You don't remember?" he asked, trying to suppress a smile but the dimple on his face concaved into something beautiful.

"No, I don't remember."

"Well, you were in the middle of a bad dream. I woke you up and you asked me to hold you, baby."

Emily thought about it for a moment and it was all starting to come back now.

"Of course I said yes," Dante continued. "I need practice getting a feel for your sleeping positions since I'm going to be your pillow for the rest of our lives."

"Dante..." Emily whispered, not knowing what else to say as she lost herself somewhere in his sweet words.

Before she could get her senses back and attempt to

put up any resistance, he'd sat up so their faces met and took her bottom lip into his mouth. He'd gotten a taste of her lips on the boat yesterday and now he wanted a taste of her tongue, of her whole, entire mouth.

Emily whimpered when she felt him pulling her down on top of him, their mouths still connected while his tongue wreaked havoc on her senses. Even though she was the one on top, his strong tongue and firm lips remained very much in control while his hand gripped the nape of her neck, holding her in place so he could fully penetrate her mouth with his tongue. Leave it up to him and he'd try to swallow her whole.

"You taste so good, baby," he managed to say after taking a quick breath – a pause more for her benefit than for his own. Shifting his body, he steadied his way in a new position – on top of her, staring down into her longing eyes.

Emily could feel his arousal pressed firmly against her leg and she instantly felt a desire to have him. Gazing into his eyes, she knew he wanted the same.

Without saying a word, he pulled her night shirt over her head, helping her to take it off, tossing it to the floor. Her bare, plump breasts lay before him, and, without wasting any time, he went for one of her breasts with his mouth while kneading the other with his hand. Soft moans escaped her lips and shivers ran down her spine with every touch. With every lick. With every suck.

"Oh, Dante," she whimpered. "Dante..."

Dante captured her tongue again, drawn to the allure of her opened mouth saying his name. She'd be saying it a lot more before the morning was over with. A lot more...

Still using his tongue, he kissed and sucked on her neck, pulling an area of skin in a suctioning way, a greedy way, then massaging the now reddish area with his tongue, feeling her body quiver underneath him. And this was just the beginning...

He traveled further, going for her breasts again. Having enjoyed them the first time around, he wanted seconds and a second helping is what he received as he greedily lapped his tongue around her breasts, feeling their softness against his taste buds. His mouth watered for more.

He licked a path to her navel, circling his tongue around it, then further down, his tongue stopped at the tip of her pajamas. It took all the willpower he had, but he stopped just shy of pulling her pajamas down and asked, "Are you sure you want to do this, Emily?"

Emily nodded. "I'm sure." Right now, she couldn't think about anything else – only this beautiful specimen hovering above her.

"I need you to be sure," he told her, still on his knees straddled over her, his manhood straining against the front of his boxers.

"I'm sure, Dante," she replied softly, gazing into his eyes.

She watched as he pulled down his boxers, his thick, mighty length demanding to be seen. She seductively bit her bottom lip as she thought about how she would be able to handle all of him. But it was too late to turn back now, not that she wanted to.

He easily removed her pajamas and felt his heart thump when he realized she wasn't wearing any panties. Then, starting from where he left off with his tongue, he begin his licks and kisses again, below her navel then down to her smooth-shaven center, lapping his tongue there, his mouth watering for a taste of her. And a taste of her he got, feeling her legs quiver at the touch of his hot tongue against her sensitive flesh.

"Dante," she whispered, instinctively grabbing his head. "Oh, Dante..."

Had he noticed she said anything? He was too busy feasting on her, wanting to send her into oblivion. Wanting to make her remember him. Needing to make her remember him.

Then she felt it – a wild, bottled up feeling of ecstasy that pressurized from her toes to her brain. She needed to release it and release it she did in one explosive, mind-boggling, pent-up shudder that made her convulse underneath the weight of him. "Oh, Dante!" she screamed. She watched him position himself between her legs and she opened them wide enough for him to nestle there perfectly.

Before she had time to brace herself, he was already priming her with the tip of his length, poking and pulling back, then sliding his shaft deep into her soul, invading her walls and forcing them to expand and stretch, recognizing his presence there. After a tight fit, their souls were connected.

Dante closed his eyes, trying to contain the feeling of being inside of her, and without a single movement, he opened them, staring down at her, the woman he'd wanted for quite some time now, but this was no conquest. And she was wrong in what she'd initially thought of him, because she wouldn't be another notch on his bedpost. He loved her, and he intended on showing her in a real action-speaks-louder-than-words type of way.

"Is something wrong?" she asked panting, noticing that he wasn't doing anything but staring down at her.

"Nothing's wrong. Everything is right. Everything is perfect. I just want to remember this moment. I don't want to rush it. I want to take my time making love to you, Emily."

With that, he bared down on her capturing her lips before parting them with his tongue and working his way into her mouth.

Emily rubbed his back with her fingertips while they kissed, while he lay buried to the hilt inside of her. His slow rocks had her ready to crumble to pieces again, so what would she do when he increased the tempo?

"Dante," she whimpered again.

His thrusts remained gentle and slow, so much so that he was able to arch his back in a way that he could lick and suck on her breasts. She steadily said his name, over and over.

Her quick breaths and the way she whispered his name turned him on. "Emily."

"Yes?"

"Don't close your eyes. I want you to see me. I want you to look at me."

"Okay."

"Take me, Emily."

"Okay, Dante," she said gasping.

"Take me. Take all of me," he ordered.

"I'm trying, baby," she panted, feeling him increase the tempo of his thrusts while never taking his eyes off of her. And she exploded again, her muscles squeezing him as her fingernails dug into his back.

"Oh, Emily," he grunted. "Oh, baby. Only you can make me feel like this. Only you can do this to me, baby," he said, letting out a loud growl, throwing his head back completely draining himself, her cave overflowing with his release.

Making love to her was incredible, beautiful and even more satisfying than he imagined it would be, so much so that he felt himself harden again, aroused even more than before.

Emily felt it too, while panting and moaning, fully intoxicated by him.

"I don't want this to end," he told her. Kissing her, parting her lips with his tongue again, he devoured more of her, feeling her legs wrap around him, sending him deeper into her abyss. Instantly, he began thrusting again. His movements were more firm, more defined than before. He was intent on giving her all she could stand.

For the third time, Emily belted his name, her body seemingly coming apart underneath him and he exploded too, more reckless than before, trying his hardest to regain control over his own body.

Completely drained and satisfied, he slowly withdrew from her body and laid next to her, holding her in his arms.

They quietly took a few breaths, recovering from rigorous lovemaking before Dante asked, "Are you okay, Emily?"

Still trying to get her breathing back to normal, she said, "Yes, I'm okay."

"Good. I know we're missing group therapy, but I'd much rather stay here with you...holding you."

"I'd rather stay here, too."

She smiled, completely spent. Dante had given her body the workout of a lifetime.

He kissed her lips, feeling her body jerk. No woman had ever made him feel this way, so turned on that he had to have more of her, so much so that his body ached for her. Even with her lying in his arms now, he could only think about the next time he would make love to her. Emily was his obsession, his paradise wife and he'd become thoroughly addicted.

Chapter 26

~ * ~

Emily crawled out of bed, feeling sore and tired after making love. Dante wasn't in the room, she noticed, and that didn't sit well with her. Where had he gone?

Melvin had never done that to her. They would make love and when she was awake, he'd be right there, asking her if she needed anything. She wanted to believe that Dante could care about her as much as Melvin had, but could he really? The truth, her truth, was that there would never be another man like Melvin. Dante had rocked her world, true enough, but look at all the things he did to ensure that they'd wind up in bed together.

And now regret was starting to creep into her mind. Why had she let Dante break down the barriers she'd built around her heart only for a few hours of pleasure on Pleasure Island? He couldn't even tell her that he loved her afterwards, which probably meant that he didn't.

Her thoughts were interrupted by her phone. It was Sherita calling again. Since she didn't get the chance to call her back yesterday, she made sure to get the call.

"Hello?" she answered, disguising her melancholy mood.

"Hey, girl. I was trying to call you yesterday."

"Is everything okay at the store?"

"No...got a notice from your landlord that the rent is

131

going up eight hundred dollars effective next month."

Emily frowned. "Are you serious?"

"Yeah...it says eight-hundred."

Emily sighed. The rent had already increased at the beginning of the year, putting her monthly lease payments to twenty-two hundred dollars. Now she would have to pay three-thousand.

"Okay, thanks for letting me know, Sherita. I'm going to call the landlord shortly. How's everything else?"

"Fine...it was pretty busy in here today."

"Okay, well if something else comes up, don't hesitate to call."

"Alrighty. Bye."

Emily hung up the phone. She couldn't bring herself to tell Sherita that she couldn't afford the new rent, but maybe if she spoke to Luke Taylor, the owner of the building that housed her store, he would consider not raising her rent. Maybe if she told him how her sales had been slacking, he'd give her some time to come up with a marketing plan to boost sales to her store. Then she'd be able to afford the rent.

That's just what she did after a long, warm shower. She called Mr. Taylor's office and asked to speak with him.

"I understand your concern," Luke said, "But I have to raise rates due to property tax hikes."

"But you just raised the rent at my store back in January."

"Yes, I'm aware of that. I also just received a property tax notification from the city."

"Mr. Taylor, I understand having a set amount of rent and making adjustments based upon taxes, but eight-hundred dollars is extreme and I simply cannot afford it right now. If you will give me time to get my sales up, I'm sure I'll be able to come up with the money."

Luke blew an agitated breath. "While I've enjoyed having your store in my building, I have a backlist of businesses who would love to lease your space for a lot more rent than I'm charging you."

"So that's what this is really about. You want to give my space away to someone else and, in order to make that happen, you drive up the lease to run me out. Well, you know what? I'll have all of my stuff out by the end of the month." Emily hung up the phone afterwards and held her head in her hands. Giving up her store would be difficult to do, but it had to be done. She had spent close to a year trying to find that location based on its convenient access and reasonable lease price of fifteen-hundred dollars, but now that the landlord was getting greedy, she had to abandon ship.

Maybe it was time to give it up. It had been more of a burden to maintain anyway. Still it kept her busy, kept her mind from being consumed with thoughts of Melvin.

She sighed and looked around the bedroom, thinking about the passionate love her and Dante had made – how he made her feel things that she'd never felt before and now, how he was gone. He wasn't even there to listen to her problems, to be of support to her. Feeling like her head was about to explode from forcing herself to hold in tears, she slid off the ring that he'd given her and placed it back on the nightstand.

Then, for the second time this morning, her phone rang. She looked at the display and saw a number she rarely ever saw but knew by heart – her father's. He'd always been distant, a man of very few words, so whenever he called, she was sure to answer.

"Hey, Dad. How are—"

Before she could say another word, he blurted out, "The ambulance is here. They're taking your mother to the hospital."

"Why? What happened?" Emily asked nervously, feeling her heart rate quicken.

"Not sure. The paramedics are checking her out now."

"Is she breathing? What happened that lead up to this?"

"She was sitting out on the patio reading one of her magazines and eating lunch. I go out there to take her some water and the next thing I know, she has a hand over her chest and was slumped over."

After a brief pause, he continued, "They're putting her on the stretcher now, so I'm going to follow them to the hospital."

"Dad, call me as soon as you get there and let me know if she ends up staying overnight. If so, I'm going to need her room number."

"Okay, sweetie."

"I'm taking the next flight out of here."

"Okay."

"And tell mom that I love her," she told him, withholding tears. When they hung up the phone, one lonely tear escaped her eye, but now wasn't the time to cry, to think about things she could've done better as a daughter instead of ignoring her parents. Now, she had to get to Jacksonville as fast as she could. She needed to be there for them.

Chapter 27

~ * ~

Dante, holding a restaurant take-out bag opened the door to the suite, ready to lay his eyes on her, his sleeping beauty. He'd gone to get lunch for the two of them since it hadn't seemed that neither one of them wanted to leave the suite today to participate in any activities. They'd found their own way to keep busy.

While getting their lunch, he ran into Steven Harris, the man he hired years ago to oversee the daily operations at the GHC resort. They chatted for a few about the testimonials the place had been getting, as well as the interest from the general public who weren't necessarily coping with loss, but wanted to stay at GHC because it was an exceptional, luxury resort. Dante had been against the idea, because he had a vision for the place and that wasn't it. However, he told Steven that once he was back at the office, he would set up a meeting so that they could discuss it further.

Dante opened the door to the bedroom where he'd left Emily sleeping and was surprised to find that she wasn't there, lying in the center of the bed where he'd left her. He checked the bathroom and she wasn't there either. Where had she gone so quickly?

He took his cell from his shirt pocket and dialed her number, then waited, anxiously listening to the rings and wondering when she would pick up. After five rings, though, it went to voicemail. He hung up and called right back, hoping that she'd answer, but again – voicemail.

He sighed and sat on the bed perplexed. That's when he noticed that her suitcase was gone.

He dialed her cell phone a third time, and when the voicemail picked up, he left a message:

Hey, Emily. It's Dante. Where are you? Call me when you get this.

He slid his phone back inside his pocket and just sat there on the bed without knowing what to do next. He didn't want to eat. As a matter of fact, he'd lost his appetite that quickly. Why would Emily wake up and just leave after the morning they'd shared? After they'd made love? He was careful not to hurt her, so why? Did she regret what happened between them? Even after her breakthrough in therapy and after making love to him this morning, had it not been enough to sway her emotions and feelings for Melvin?

Dante stood up from the bed and in a bout of anger and frustration, he grabbed the bag of food and slung it across the room, its contents spilling out onto the floor. Just when he thought he'd had her where he wanted her, she up and disappeared on him. To make matters worse, he looked over at the nightstand and saw the ring.

Chapter 28

~ * ~

After a layover in Atlanta, she finally arrived to Jacksonville where she'd took a taxi to the hospital. If something happened to her mother and she hadn't had the chance to apologize, she would never forgive herself for being intentionally distant.

At the hospital, she raced to her mother's second floor room, pushed the door open and saw her lying on the bed. Her eyes were closed.

Her father had been sitting next to the bed and rose up from his seat when Emily burst into the room.

"Dear, please don't wake her," he said. "She just came out of surgery a few hours ago and the doctors just want her to rest."

"Oh my gosh, Dad," Emily said, rushing around the bed and finding herself in her father's embrace.

"It's okay, honey."

"No, it's not," she cried. "I'm an awful daughter. I should've been here."

"You can't blame yourself for this, Emily."

"Yes I can, because I should know about mom's health problems. I just became so consumed by Melvin's death that I forgot about the people who are still alive – people who love and need me."

"Well, you're here now aren't you honey? And guess what?"

"Yeah?"

"Today is a good day to begin again."

Emily smiled through her sadness. Her father had always told her that as a child. Begin again. How true that was. She couldn't go back and change the years she'd wasted avoiding her parents. All she could do was start over.

"What did the doctor say about her recovery?" Emily asked, staring at her sleeping mother.

Her father walked up next to her and said, "He said she'll make a full recovery, but it's going to take quite a while before she's back to herself again."

Emily pondered how she might be able to help her parents, especially since they were in Florida and she was in North Carolina. Then again, she was closing the store for good. What else would she be sticking around for if she stayed in Asheville?

Chapter 29

~ * ~

The next day, Dante walked around the resort dumbfounded, trying to figure out what had happened between himself and Emily. He tried to call her several more times this morning, but still, she hadn't answered. Then he got an idea – call her boutique. She had mentioned to him that her friend Sherita was running the store in her absence. Maybe she knew where Emily had run off to.

He Googled the store number on his phone, then dialed it.

"Emily's Boutique, may I help you?"

"Hi. Is this Sherita?"

"This is she? Who's speaking?"

"This is Dante Champion. I'm a friend of—"

"Oh, hi, Dante."

He frowned. "You know me?"

"Yeah. Emily told me about you."

That made him feel good, but didn't do anything to give him any sort of indication where Emily was. He told her, "Emily left the resort yesterday afternoon and I haven't been able to reach her. Would you by any chance know where she might be?"

Sherita thought for a moment and said, "No. I don't. I did speak to her yesterday about the store, though."

"You did?"

"Yeah."

"About what time?"

"Um...must've been around one."

"Did she seem upset at all?"

"No. Well, I take that back...she was a little upset about the rent increase."

"Rent increase?"

"Yeah. I got the notice from the landlord about a rent increase and I told her about it."

"Oh..."

"You said she left yesterday afternoon?" Sherita inquired.

"Yes, and I have not been able to get in contact with her and have no idea where she might be."

"Hmm..." Sherita said, brainstorming a moment. If Emily left, it must've been for a good reason. Then she thought of a perfect solution. "I'll call her and tell her that you're looking for her because I honestly don't know where she is either."

"Thank you. I appreciate that."

"I can call you back at this number?" she asked.

"Yes. This is my cell."

"All right. I'm going to get off the phone and call her now. If I get her on the phone, I'll call you back and let you know. If she doesn't answer, then I won't bother calling you back."

"Okay. Thanks again."

"You're welcome.

While Dante appreciated Sherita's efforts, he wanted to be the one in control of the situation, not sitting on the sidelines waiting for a phone call. So he did the next best thing he knew to do – he called the hotel where her friend Melanie worked. Since he used the site for several business functions, he'd already had the number programmed into his phone.

"Guest services. Melanie Summers speaking."

"Hi Melanie. This is Dante Champion."

"Hi, Mr. Champion. Looking to book another meeting here?"

"Not at the moment. The reason for my call is a personal one."

"Personal how?"

"I'm looking for Emily. She's a friend of yours if I'm not mistaken."

"Yes she is."

"I don't know if she told you about the mass wedding at the resort this weekend—"

"Yes, she told me all about it."

"Well, yesterday afternoon, she left and I have no idea where she is. Would you by any chance know where she is?"

Melanie hadn't responded. She had spoken with Emily this morning and had known where Emily was – in Jacksonville with her sick mother. And Emily had also told her how she thought the time she'd spent with Dante had been a mistake. Melanie didn't want to hear that from her because she knew Dante was the perfect man for Emily. Still, Emily wasn't sure of what she wanted. Melvin had her heart.

After a relatively long period of silence, Dante said, "Melanie, if you know where she is, please tell me. I'm worried about her."

Melanie sighed. "I don't know if it's my place to get in the middle of you two, Mr. Champion, so—"

"Melanie, please. I need to know where she is."

Melanie still hadn't responded. She knew Dante had deep feelings for Emily. She could hear it in his voice. The only problem was, Emily wasn't convinced. If she was, she had a good way of pretending she wasn't falling for him. "She's in Jacksonville, Florida. Her mother had a heart attack and she left the resort to be with her and her father."

Dante's heart sank. He was relieved that she was

okay, but felt sorry for her mother and for Emily to have to go through that.

"Thanks for letting me know. I appreciate it."

"Oh, and Dante..." she said, foregoing the formality of calling him Mr. Champion.

"Yes?"

"If you love her, you really need to be patient because she's still not over Melvin's death. I know you know that, and I also know that trying to love someone who won't love you back is tiring, but Emily really needs you."

"I know. Thank you, Melanie. I owe you." As soon as Dante ended the call, he made plans to be picked up by the company jet. He'd see Emily today. He wanted nothing other than to be there for her through this distressing time in her life.

Chapter 30

~ * ~

Later in the evening, Emily was walking from the cafeteria with two cups of coffee – one for her and her father – when she saw Dante walking towards her.

Dang-it, Melanie! She wanted to scream, regretting the fact that she told Melanie where she had gone. How else would Dante know because she surely hadn't told anyone else.

Emily was so nervous, she almost dropped the coffee when she saw him walking towards her, wearing a pair of dark jeans and a camel colored jacket that matched his leather shoes and plaid shirt.

"Hi," he told her when he'd gotten a little closer.

"What are you doing here, Dante?"

Her question took him aback. "What do you mean? My wife is here and I wanted to be here with you, to help you, Emily."

"No. I don't want you here. I want you to leave."

"Emily, I'm not leaving. I want to be here for you," he repeated.

"No. Leave. I don't want or need you here. Goodbye." She continued walking pass him like he wasn't even standing there.

Dante turned around and said, "What did I do to deserve this?" still watching her walk away from him.

He sighed and threw his hands up in the air. Instead of causing a scene, he returned to the end of the hallway and took a seat in the waiting area. He removed the wedding ring he'd given her from his shirt pocket and twirled it in between his thumb and index fingers. Emily meant too much to him only for him to walk away now. She'd penetrated too deep inside of his heart.

He stood up and headed for Emily's mother's room. It was time for the Mitchells to know that they had a son-in-law. Once there, he tapped on the door then proceeded into the room like he was family. Well, he was family. He was Emily's husband. Her parent's son-in-law.

Emily's eyes nearly popped out of her head when she saw Dante step in the room.

"What are—" she began.

"Mr. Mitchell," he said interrupting Emily before she had a chance to silence him. "I'm Dante Champion, your daughter's husband.

"Husband?" her father responded, holding the cup of coffee in his right hand. He looked at Emily, wearing a frown like it was a crown.

"Emily, what is this man talking about?"

"Dad, I can explain, but first, I need to speak with Dante in the hallway, okay." She walked pass them both to reach the door.

Dante followed her into the hallway.

"What on God's green earth do you think you're doing?" she asked with a hand on her hip.

"I'm being here for you. I told you that."

"You must have it twisted. I told you to leave, Dante."

"I heard what you said. Now, you hear me—"

"No, no, no! Stop talking."

"No. Don't tell me to stop talking, Emily."

"You got some nerve. Why are you even here? Thought you were done with me."

His frown deepened. "Done with you?"

"Yeah. Done." She crossed her arms. "You had sex with me and I woke up and you were gone."

"Correction...I made love to you and the reason I was *gone*, as you put it, is because I went to get us some lunch. You knew I hadn't left. My suitcases were where they've been since we arrived at the resort. Come on, Emily. What is this really about?"

"I can't talk to you right now."

"Emily, you're still my wife and I thought everything between us these past few days were going good. So tell me...are you having second thoughts? Regrets? Is that what's really going on here?"

"I have to get back to my parents."

"Okay, since you want to play that game. I'm right behind you."

Emily took a deep breath and sighed. It was going to be a long night.

Chapter 31

~ * ~

"Let's take a walk, Dante, if you don't mind," Emily's father, George, told him.

"Sure," Dante replied.

Emily was lying in the chair next to her mother. Both women were sleeping. A nurse had just stopped by to check her mother's vitals.

"I know we didn't officially meet, and I apologize for my rudeness, but I had no idea that Emily had gotten married. At any rate, I'm George. My wife's name is Antoinette." After shaking hands, George said, "So how did you meet my daughter?"

"I met her at a festival but we got to know each other on a website."

"What kind of website?"

"It's called Grieving Hearts Connect...a website where people who lost spouses in death can connect with each other."

"Oh, I see. So you must know all about Melvin, huh?"

"Yes, Sir. I do."

"He was a good man. If I could've hand-picked a husband for my daughter, it would've been him. He loved Emily very much."

"As do I, Sir."

George looked at him. "Emily told me she would never remarry, so I'm curious about what made her marry you."

"Must be love," Dante replied, but he wasn't too sure if Emily loved him or not.

George grinned. "I'm a very observant man, Dante, and when you came into the room, my daughter frowned. It was obvious that she didn't want you there. And she wasn't wearing a ring, either. You want to tell me what's *really* going on?"

Dante stopped walking when he noticed that George had. "Sure. I'll tell you what's going on. I love your daughter. We were married two weeks ago on a beach with many other couples and we were basically giving the marriage a two-week trial. She left early to come here to be with her mother."

"Why didn't you come with her?"

"Because I didn't know she had left. She didn't tell me she was leaving. She just dropped everything and came here, and when I found out, I dropped everything to be here with her. And I intend to be there for her always, to take care of her."

"Not too sure about that, son. My daughter is very strong-willed and stubborn. She dedicated herself to Melvin, and..." he shook his head. "When Melvin passed, Emily put her life on hold. She stopped talking to me and her Mother and I think the only thing that has kept her from having a breakdown is that little boutique of hers. She invested every dime of money Melvin left behind to the store because he'd helped her in the early stages of it, you know, when she'd first got the idea to open a boutique."

Dante nodded. Now he understood her attachment to the store, keeping it running and making it a success.

"Tell me more about yourself, Dante." The men had made their way outside and sat on one of the concrete benches.

"Well, not sure exactly what you want to know,

so...ah... I was married for five years and my wife passed. We didn't have any children. It was just me and her."

"Do you want children? I know Emily does...well, she used to."

"Yes. I want children."

"What do you do for work, Dante?"

"I own The Champion Corporation. We specialize in creating web companies."

"An entrepreneur..."

"Yes, Sir."

"Ain't nothing wrong with that. Do you live in Asheville?"

"Yes. I moved there from San Francisco."

"You think you'll ever go back?"

"Nah. My life is in Asheville. My brothers live there too, and Emily has her store there, so..."

"Yeah, she has it for now at least. She told me she was having trouble with the landlord raising the rent."

"Really?" Dante said like this was the first time he'd heard this. Sherita had initially told him about the trouble that Emily was having with the landlord, but in order to see if he could get even more information from George, he played dumb.

"Yeah, she was talking about possibly closing the store and moving here to Jacksonville. It was nothing set in stone...just casual conversation. She's pretty upset about the store and worried about her mother."

"That's understandable."

"Well, I'm going to get back in there and check on my girls. I hope Emily changes her mind about you, Dante. You seem like a decent man."

"Thank you, Sir."

Once George was further away from him, Dante took out his cell and called Dimitrius at the office.

"What's up, Dante?"

"Listen, Dimitrius...I don't have much time, but I need a huge favor."

"What's that?"

"I need you to find out who owns the building where Emily has her boutique. It's the same building as that Caribbean restaurant you like."

"Okay, Dante. I'm on it."

"When you get the name and number, text it to me."

"Will do."

"Okay. Later.

Chapter 32

~ * ~

Emily's mother, Antionette, opened her eyes and smiled at her daughter.

"How do you feel, mom?"

"Feel like I've been run over by a city bus, child, but you know your mom is a survivor."

Emily smiled. Her mother was a tough woman. She liked that very much about her.

"Mom, what do you think about me staying with you and dad for a couple of weeks?"

"I think that will be nice, but I know you have your own life, dear."

Not so much. Emily didn't have much of a life these days, but her mother didn't need to know that.

"It'll be fine."

"But what about Dante?" her father inquired.

"Dante?" her mother asked, her eyes bright. "Who's Dante?"

"Uh...um..." Emily stammered.

"Dante is Emily's husband," her father blurted out.

Antionette's eyes grew even bigger. "Husband? You got married, Emily?"

"Ma, calm down before you hurt yourself. Please."

"Emily, you have a husband?" Antionette inquired again.

Before she could answer, Dante came in the room with coffee and a bag.

"Hi. Good morning," he said when he saw that Antionette was awake. He set the coffee and bagels on the countertop and walking over near the bed, he said, "It's nice to meet you, Mrs. Mitchell. How are you feeling?"

"I'm feeling a lot better now."

Dante smiled. "I'm Dante."

"Nice to meet you, Dante. You have to excuse my demeanor, but Emily neglected to tell us that she remarried."

"Dante, please let her rest," Emily said.

"I'm fine dear," Antionette spoke up. "I'm just in a state of shock to find out that I have a new son-in-law." Antionette looked at Dante again and asked, "You said your name was Dante?"

"Yes, ma'am."

"When did you marry my daughter?"

"About two weeks ago."

"Oh my word...I didn't even know Emily was seeing anyone. But you are a welcomed sight, I tell you that. Emily swore up and down that she would never remarry after Melvin. I'm sure you know all about Melvin."

Emily sighed into her palms then said, "Ma..."

"What dear? I'm excited. Why didn't you tell me you married his handsome man?"

"Because we're not—"

"Looks like I'm going to have me some grandbabies after all," Antoinette said, interrupting her.

Emily frowned, stood up and walked out of the room in a hurry.

"I'll be right back," Dante said to Emily's parents before leaving to room to go after her. He looked to the right, then to the left and saw her dash around the corner.

"Emily," he yelled loud enough so she would hear him. Then he jogged to catch up to her, finding her sitting in the waiting room, her face buried in her hands. "Emily," he said, kneeling in front of her.

She hadn't looked at him, just remained as she was.

He placed his hands on her knees. "Emily—"

"Haven't you humiliated me enough? Please go. Leave me and my family alone."

"Baby, I'm just trying to be here for you."

"I don't want you here," she said with a shaky, broken voice. "I want you to leave me alone!"

Dante wanted to do nothing other than grab her into his arms and console her, to show her how much she needed him. But he was tired of fighting for a woman who didn't want him. So instead, he stood up, sucked in a breath and said, "You can't say I didn't try." Then he walked away.

Chapter 33

~ * ~

On the company jet during his flight home, he dialed the number that Dimitrius had texted to him – the landlord to the building where Emily's boutique was located.

"Hello," a woman answered.

"Hi. This is Dante Champion calling. I'm looking for Luke Taylor."

"Please hold and I'll check to see if he's available for you."

"Thanks."

"You're welcome."

After listening to some instrumentals for a few seconds, he heard a male voice on the other end.

"Luke Taylor. What can I do for you?"

"I'm interested in buying the building you own, located on Battery Park Avenue."

"Well, I'll stop you right there. That location isn't for sale and—"

"Eight million," Dante said.

"Excuse me?"

"I said eight million. Now I've done my research, so I know the building is only worth five million, but I'm willing to throw in an extra three million for your trouble."

Luke thought about it for a moment and said, "I'll think on it and let you know. I'm not sure what you want with the building, but I'm contractually liable to the current tenants who've set up shop there, so if, and that's a big if, I were to take you up on your offer, we would have to come to the table and figure out a plan for the current tenants to vacate."

"That won't be a problem. I do not plan on making anyone move out."

"Hmm. Okay. Well, I'll still give your proposal some thought."

"Don't think too long. The offer is off the table tomorrow at noon.

"Then you'll be hearing from me before noon tomorrow then, Mr. Champion."

"Good. I'll be waiting for your call."

Chapter 34

~ * ~

Two weeks later, Emily returned home after being in Jacksonville. Her mother had been doing much better and she felt confident that she would be okay now. She hadn't spoken to Dante in those two weeks – no text messages, instant messages, phone calls, nothing. Since she was back home today, she wanted to go by the boutique and collect a few more pieces of her merchandise. Sherita had already began boxing up some things and was going to meet her there this morning.

When she pulled up and parked in front of the store, Emily saw Sherita's car already there. Emily got out of the car, in tears. The store already had cardboard paper in the windows.

Sherita hugged her tight and said, "It's okay, Emily."

"No, it's not okay," Emily cried. "I was supposed to make this store a success and I failed. My life has been nothing but a series of failures...one disappointment after another."

"No, that's not true. You have a lot to be proud of, Emily."

Emily wiped her eyes. "Like what?"

"You have your health...your parents..."

Emily batted more tears away and said, "Let's just go in and see what else I need to remove. You said you got most of the clothes out, right?"

Sherita nodded. Then she unlocked the door. Emily couldn't see the smile on Sherita's face since she was standing behind her, but Emily was about to get the surprise of a lifetime.

When Sherita opened the door, more tears poured out of Emily's eyes. The place had been completely redone. Whoever leased the space must've had money, because she couldn't afford to tile the floor in black and white, or add two additional dressing rooms and completely cover a small portion of the wall with a floor-to-ceiling mirror. The register was even computerized with a barcode system. "I can't believe somebody already moved in," she whimpered.

Melanie came walking from the back and said, "Actually, this is your place, Em...completely redone."

Emily looked confused. "What? What are you doing here, Melanie?"

"Well, since I helped to design the place, I figured I should be here to surprise you."

"But...but...how? You know I can't afford this place."

"Well, thanks to a gentleman by the name of Dante Champion, you won't have to."

"What do you mean?"

"When he found out what the landlord had been doing to you by raising the rent, he bought the building."

"What?"

Melanie smiled big. "You heard me. Your husband bought this building."

More tears fell from her eyes.

"And since you're not talking to him, he wanted me to let you know that you'll never have to pay a lease for this place even if you never speak to him again. It's yours."

Emily sniffled and dabbed her nose.

"Listen, Emily," Melanie said. "I don't know what

happened between you guys, but Dante is a good man and he's completely in love with you. I think you owe it to him to give the marriage a try."

Emily squeezed her eyes tight. "You're right, but..."

"But what?" Sherita asked. "Girl, if I had a man do something like this for me, I would be at his crib right now."

"It's more complicated than that. I messed up big time. I was a complete jerk to him when he came to the hospital."

"Why?" Sherita inquired.

"Because I felt myself falling so deeply in love with him that it scared me. I thought I could only have those feelings for Melvin, but—"

"Well, all I know is, even after your little hospital meltdown, Dante called me personally to get ideas on what you might like for the store," Melanie said. "He was very exact, and knew what he wanted this place to look like for you."

He had some idea what she wanted. They had talked about it briefly, well, when they were talking. Little did she know that he was listening intently, and was maybe even already making plans to help her with the store.

"After everything I put him through, he still did this for me. I really don't even know what to say."

"I'm sure a simple 'thank you' would be a start," Melanie said. "You have to start somewhere, Em, or lose another good man."

Emily shook her head. "I think it might be too late."

Chapter 35

~ * ~

A week later, Dante was sitting behind his desk, his brothers in his office again, having their weekly meeting. Even though it was difficult to do, he tried to push Emily to the back of his mind. Business had to resume as usual and he had to get back into the swing of things if he was going to move on and live without her.

"First on the agenda," Dante began, "Is filling the position of Marketing Manager, someone to oversee the bulk of the marketing team and, who would report directly to Desmond. As we discussed a few weeks ago, that would free up some time for Desmond to do more traveling."

"Have you posted the position internally yet?" Desmond asked.

"No. I don't need to post it. I have a candidate in mind that I would like to discuss with the both of you."

"And who's that?" Dimitrius asked.

"Melanie Summers."

"The chick from the hotel?" Desmond asked.

"The *woman* from the hotel who works in guest services. Yes," Dante said. "She's very sharp, professional and I think she'll make an impact on the marketing team."

"Cool. I would *love* for her to work under me," Desmond said with a sneaky grin.

Dante watched Dimitrius grimace at Desmond's

comments. Then he asked him, "What do you think, Dimitrius?"

"I think we should bring her in for a group interview," Dimitrius suggested.

Desmond frowned. "A group interview? She'll be reporting to me. I'm capable of handling my own interviews."

"Des, I think Dimitrius is right," Dante said. He knew Dimitrius had a thing for Melanie, which is probably the reason he requested a group interview. That would ensure he'd be part of the process and thus have time to interact with her. "I haven't spoken with her about it yet. I plan on speaking to her sometime this week and if she shows an interest, I'll set up the interview. So moving on to the next item on the agenda...three weeks ago when I was at the GHC resort, I briefly ran into Steven Harris. He brought up something that Desmond had mentioned a while ago...about how there seems to be interest at the resort from people who are not grieving the loss of a spouse or needing help from therapists per se. These are just everyday folk, looking to vacation at a high-end, exclusive resort and as you know, GHC is just that. Desmond, do you have any thoughts?"

"Steven is right. The interest is there, and as you know, autumn and winter are our slowest seasons. So I was thinking about exploring the idea and making those months available for *outsiders*, shall we say."

Dante nodded and said, "Dimitrius, you want to weigh in on this?"

Dimitrius rubbed his chin and said, "Um...I was thinking about how that would work from an accounts perspective, because if these *outsiders* don't fit the model, then they have no need in opening an account, so we will lose money from the monthly subscriptions."

"That's a good point," Dante said. "But we could

recoup the money as a premium upon booking, can't we?"

"We could. However, the system is not set up like that currently."

"Well, that's not a problem. We can get I.T. to do a system change if need be. I'm just worried about the brand. Right now, as it stands, GHC is strictly for the purpose of rehabilitating and helping people. If we change that and let any and everybody in, then I think we will lose our credibility, and people who really need the help of the services offered there may turn elsewhere...someplace they deem to be more *serious* than GHC."

"I could see something like that happening," Dimitrius concurred.

"And that's my main concern, which I have expressed to Steven," Dante said. "I didn't create GHC to be a vacation resort. I created it to be sort of a grief retreat...someplace that could serve as a springboard for new beginnings."

"Too bad it doesn't work for everyone," Dimitrius said, totally off subject.

"What's that supposed to mean?" Dante asked.

"Just what I said. It doesn't work for everyone."

"GHC works, Dimitrius. You know that. You've read the testimonials and—"

"You were there for almost two full weeks," Dimitrius said. "Where's your new beginning, Dante?"

"*My* new beginning?" Dante asked, completely caught off guard by what his brother was hinting at.

"Yeah, meaning, have you heard from her?" Dimitrius asked, referring to Emily.

"As you know, I just got back into town last night after attending a business summit in Indianapolis."

"So the answer is no?" Desmond inquired.

Dante sighed. "Let's get back to work."

"Let's not," Desmond responded. "Dante, I've watched you immerse yourself in this company and make it the success that it is, but I know you were only doing it to keep Anita off of your mind, and now, you're doing the same with Emily. You can't keep on doing this to yourself."

Dante leaned back in his chair. He missed Emily, but he didn't want to pursue a woman who was dead set on being alone and miserable for the rest of her life. After a few more seconds, he finally spoke up and said, "Emily has made it clear to me that I'm not the man she wants."

"Then why'd you spend millions of dollars buying that building so she wouldn't lose her store?" Dimitrius asked.

"Because I love her and I want her to be happy."

"And she knows that?" Dimitrius asked. He told Dante before to tell Emily how he really felt, that he loved her.

Dante, however, had never said those words to Emily because he wasn't sure if she felt the same way about him. If judging by actions, Emily should've known that he loved her, but when it came down to love, there was nothing like having those three little words spoken to you by someone whom you have the exact same feelings for – the same affection.

"We still have several more items on the agenda to discuss. I suggest we get back to work," Dante told his brothers, finally quieting them.

Chapter 36

~ * ~

Dante had been frustrated for the remainder of the workday, because he was sure that after the good deed he did for Emily, he would at least have gotten a phone call from her. But she chose to remain distant and that upset him. To make matters worse, all he could do was think about her, about how they'd made passionate love and how she was irate with him at the hospital.

At home now, he glanced at the clock. It was 1:04 a.m., just after midnight and he couldn't sleep. He decided to go the kitchen for a drink. He poured some Bourbon in a glass, then sat on a barstool at the island. He tossed it all to the back of his throat and remembered being deep inside of her, making love to her, but the thought was tainted by her telling him to leave the hospital – telling him she didn't need him, that she wanted him to leave her alone when all he wanted to do was love her.

The chime of the doorbell interrupted his thoughts and brought a frown to his face. He looked at the clock again. Who was at his door at this time of night?"

Wearing only a pair of boxers, he sauntered to the door, then peeped out of the blinds. There she was, Emily, the woman who had caused him so much heartache. The woman of his dreams. The woman who invaded his life with her personality and natural beauty. The woman who was able to excite his heart and make him do things he'd never done before. She had also turned out to be the woman who pained him.

He opened the door and Emily looked him up and down, having flashbacks of the one and only time they'd made love. Dante had been incredible, she could admit. He was strong and caring, there for her emotionally, only she refused to accept the emotional part. She'd pushed him away and now she hoped that she hadn't pushed him too far, so far that he couldn't stand the sight of her.

"Hi," she forced out.

Had Dante heard that she'd spoken? He was startled by the fact that she was even there, at his house. She'd never been there before. Just the feeling of her being at his home was enough to excite him, to make him believe that love between them was possible. But she'd proven that love isn't what she wanted. She wanted to be left alone. So why was she standing here, at his door at such a late hour?

One thing was for sure. He was done with her hot-and-cold attitude. One minute she couldn't stand him. The other, she was kissing him, screaming his name louder than he'd ever heard a woman do it and then she was back to hating him again. Not anymore. It was his turn to take control.

"Why are you here, Emily?"

She crossed her arms as if a sudden chill had struck her.

"I just wanted to talk."

"At one-thirty in the morning, you want to talk?"

"Yes. I wanted to apologize to you for the way I acted."

Just taking in her beauty had his heart pounding in his chest. She had on a black, flowey dress that fell at her knees. Her curly hair that he loved so much was bouncy and neat. He remembered his fingers submerged in those curls while they'd made love.

"Why are you here, Emily?" he asked again, watching her lips tremble.

"Dante, I'm sorry about the things I said to you. You didn't deserve them and—"

"And what? You want me to forgive you and then what happens, Emily? You get angry again...regret everything we do together, push me away like I mean nothing to you?"

"No."

"Well, that's what you did, and I would never do that to you, Emily. Never!"

Tears blurred her vision. He was upset and now, she knew it was too late. She shouldn't have allowed so much time to pass between them. The distance only made things worse. "I don't know what happens now, Dante," she said. "I just wanted you to know that I'm sorry." She covered her face and turned away from him, heading back for her car.

Before she could walk away, he stepped out onto the porch and grabbed her forearm, pulling her into his grasp, staring into her worried eyes while holding her head between those strong hands of his. "Why are you here, Emily?"

More tears spilled out of her eyes as she looked at him. With trembling lips, she said, "Because...because I miss you and I love you, Dante."

He closed his eyes briefly. Hearing her say those words gave him a euphoric feeling even more than when they made love. He longed to hear them and finally, she was able to confess what he had known. She loved him.

Dante attacked her lips, kissing her hungrily, sucking greedily on them and parting them with his tongue so he could reacquaint himself with her taste. Just the sensation of their warm tongues touching made him want to explode.

Before either of them knew what was happening, because it all happened so spontaneously, Emily was in the foyer, pinned up against the wall, Dante's taut, muscular, naked body holding her there so tightly, she could hardly breathe. He wasted no time removing her panties, nearly ripping them in the process. He needed to be inside of her now and not a moment longer. After sliding his boxers to the floor, his manhood throbbing in anticipation, he settled perfectly inside of her after a few priming pumps.

"Oh, baby," he said. Being inside of her felt good, too good. Immeasurably good. He could never feel this way with any other woman and that's how he knew Emily was *it* for him. She was 'the one' and he loved her. He'd always loved her.

Feeling himself losing control and still thrusting while holding her up with the strength of one hand, he used the other to snatch her dress over her head, messing up her hair in the process. But that didn't matter. Once they made it to the bedroom, her curls were as good as gone.

Their lips connected again. Emily locked her legs tighter around his waist. That gave him an even better penetrating angle. Made him go even deeper if that was possible. While their tongues entangled, she moaned and grunted, feeling every pull of his member against her insides.

Dante felt her muscles tighten around him, squeeze him while her fingernails dug into his flesh as she moved her mouth away from his so she could belt out a scream that his neighbors could hear.

"Dante!"

He threw his head back when he'd heard her scream his name. Oh, how intoxicating it was to hear the sound of her sweet voice call out his name. It was just as exciting as being deep inside of her body, loving her and wanting to please her. At the same time, he needed this, needed her and hearing her satisfied had him over the edge. His face had turned a shade darker when his pleasure finally arrived, washing over them.

"Emily!"

Their gazes met and Dante kissed her lips. While their faces were a breath apart, he said, "I love you."

"I love you too, Dante."

"Good, because I need to take you to my bedroom so we can start all over again," he told her and he'd still had her pinned at the wall. Still inside of her.

Emily wanted to respond but all she could do was stare into his eyes. Her words were caught at the back of her throat.

With their souls still connected, her legs still wrapped around him, hanging on for dear life, he slowly ascended the spiral staircase, only breaking their gazes to guide her safely into the bedroom and on his bed – the same bed where, just a short while ago, he couldn't sleep. Now he had a good reason not to sleep. He'd be making love to his wife, for the first time in his bed. Their bed. Their home.

"I missed you, Emily," he said in a whisper, their noses touching.

She felt him harden inside of her even more when he'd spoken those words. She knew they were true, because he hadn't even wanted to separate from her, keeping their bodies joined while coming up the stairs and landing on his bed. "I missed you too, Dante."

Lowering himself to her again, his tongue took a deep plunge into her mouth, kissing her with so much precision and greed that her toes curled.

Her hands gripped the nape of his neck and massaged him there and at his shoulders, while he tried with all his might to consume her.

He massaged her breasts, tasting her there and when

he felt her thighs tighten and heard the deep moan come from her throat, he knew her pleasure, the pleasure he was delivering to her, was bound to come all over again.

She slammed her eyelids together, trying her best to handle him, his strength and his stamina, feeling her legs stiffen, then quiver as everything in the room seemed to have been spinning out of control.

"Oh, Dante!"

And just after she'd completely fell apart, so did he, groaning and shuddering on top of her. Not once did he close his eyes. He wanted to see her, take her all in, the same way she was taking him. All of him.

Dante then positioned himself beside of her after disconnecting their bodies, but not their hearts. He looked upon her adoringly, stroking curls away from her face, something he liked to do, she noticed.

"Emily?"

"Yes?"

"I really do want this."

"I know."

"And I need you to be all-in because, as you know, I'm very decisive. I've always been that way. I know what I want. I want you, and when I love, I love hard, baby. I need you to understand that."

"I understand," she said softly.

"Tell me what you want."

She smiled. "I want to be happy. I want to be with you, share meals with you, wake up every morning to you and eat oysters with you."

He smiled.

So did she. "I don't know if I ever thanked you for what you did with the store. It's beautiful. I appreciate it very much."

"I know how much the store meant to you and I wanted you to keep it, even if you didn't want to keep me."

"I do want to keep you. I love you."

"Good, because I need you to move in with me immediately. No more pushing me away. If we're going to do this, we need to do it right. Agreed?"

"Agreed."

"And I want us to start working on our family right away."

She smiled. "We've already started on that. I'm not on any sort of birth control, Dante."

That made him happy, more than she could ever imagine. He'd always wanted children, a legacy – some babies to further his empire. A son to groom. A daughter to adore, as much as he adored her mother.

He leaned forward to kiss her sweet, juicy lips again. "I promise that, when you open your eyes in the morning, I'll be here, staring into them, waiting to make love to you."

Her lips curved into a smile as she stared into the depth of his eyes. After getting to know him so well, that was a promise she knew he'd keep. And she'd keep him, forever and love him forever, the same way he loved her.

* * * * *

Also by Tina Martin:

Accidental Deception, The Accidental Series, Book 1
Accidental Heartbreak, The Accidental Series, Book 2
Accidental Lovers, The Accidental Series, Book 3
What Donovan Wants, The Accidental Series, Book 4

Dying To Love Her
Dying To Love Her 2
Dying To Love Her 3

The Millionaire's Arranged Marriage (The Alexanders, Book 1)
Watch Me Take Your Girl (The Alexanders, Book 2)
Her Premarital Ex (The Alexanders, Book 3)
The Object of His Obsession (The Alexanders, Book 4)

Secrets On Lake Drive
Can't Just Be His Friend
The Baby Daddy Interviews
Just Like New to the Next Man
Vacation Interrupted
The Crush

Read book descriptions, excerpts and more at
www.tinamartin.net

ABOUT THE AUTHOR

Tina Martin is the bestselling author of romantic suspense and women's fiction novels. Her books include, The Dying To Love Her Series, The Accidental Series, The Alexander Series, The Champion Brothers Series, Secrets On Lake Drive, Can't Just Be His Friend, The Baby Daddy Interviews, Just Like New to the Next Man, Might As Well Be Single, The Crush and Vacation Interrupted.

She resides in Charlotte, North Carolina with her husband and two young children. Visit www.tinamartin.net for information on upcoming novels as well as excerpts and book trailers.